BREATHLESS
Kathryn J. Bain

---

1.   http://www.kathrynjbain.com

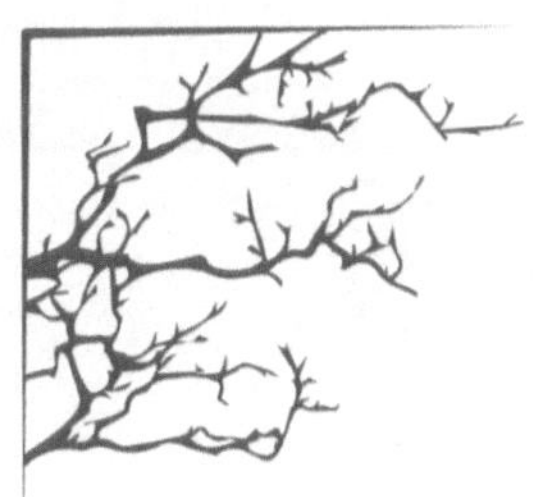

Dedication

I'd like to thank all my critique group partners who are constantly showing me I'm never finished when I think I am. Thanks to my family for their patience while I fulfill my life's dream.

To receive updates regarding upcoming releases, book signings, new releases, craft festivals, or speaking engagements, visit www.kathrynjbain.com[2] to sign up for my newsletter.

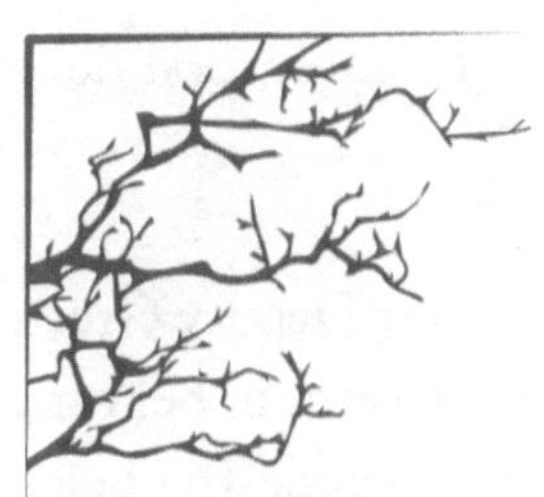

1

The police finally left, and neighbors returned to their own lives. Only Lydia Frederickson remained. Discomfort crawled into her. Why did she call over such a trivial thing as a prank phone call? But when the voice described what she was wearing, she allowed her fear to rule. She pulled her knees to her chest as she sat in the plush chair next to the window. Lydia couldn't get his unsettling words from her mind.

"I want you," he'd taunted, his breathing loud and quick. "I can feel you near me in that pretty, pink gown. So nice to touch. I bet you're nice to touch, too."

The last two evenings, it had only been dead air. Tonight, he said disturbing things.

She glanced at the notepad. *Phone with caller ID, also feature that blocks calls without identifying numbers*, it read. Deputy Green had made the suggestions, telling her it might end the calls. She prayed he was right.

Her queen-sized bed welcomed her as she coiled in the safety of the blankets. The house had an eerie silence she hadn't noticed before. She longed for Justin's reassurance as she scooted closer to the center. Her hand jutted out to reach for him, but the pillow on the other side lay bare, as empty and lonely as when her husband died almost two years ago. Sadness overwhelmed her as she fought to hold the tears in. She missed the comfort and safety of him next to her.

What was that? Lydia bolted upright. Was it her imagination or was the caller in the house? Deputy Green said he checked, but the creep could have been hiding. He might be downstairs. Her heart stuck in her throat as she listened for any sound showing his presence. She

1

raced to the bedroom door and clicked the lock. The cold wood door added to her shivers as she pressed her ear to it.

Nothing.

She recalled checking all the locks downstairs after Deputy Green left. Even with that reassurance, her pulse continued to race in her ears.

"How did he know what I had on?" Lydia whispered. The beige walls held no answers. The pink gown lay in the middle of the bathroom floor. A pair of shorts and a t-shirt now covered her.

Why now? Why so near the anniversary of Justin's death? While seated on the edge of the bed, she grasped the picture frame. It held a smiling Justin on their wedding day, his arms surrounding her. She went to the closet and swung open the door. His suits and shirts were neatly hung on the right side. She found the purple long-sleeved shirt and pulled it into her chest. It's fabric soft as when he wore it last. The warmth of his aroma cradled her.

She returned to the bed and moved closer to Justin's side, clutching both the photograph and the shirt against her body. This time nothing kept the tears from falling.

A cat screeched outside, startling her from her sobs. She tightened the covers and shoved hair from her dampened face.

"God," she pleaded to the ceiling. "Please help me through the next few days."

MATTHEW WINTERS REVVED the Harley Davidson Ultra Classic motorcycle. He'd searched a long time for the ultimate ride. When he saw the two-tone, black and smoke gold color, it summoned him as if hypnotized. The Classics were popular, so he snatched it up the day he came across it without quibbling over price. He had more than enough saved to pay cash.

The sun had risen about an hour earlier this Saturday morning to combine with a light cool breeze that made him glad he wore his FXRG leather jacket. Dampness covered the ground from the sprinkling of rain that had fallen before dawn.

He grinned, wondering what waited for him at his new job. According to his friend Riley Owens, most of the citizens held a somewhat conservative view of things. Did that mean more than just their political opinions? Keeping people on their toes. It's what Matthew did best. There might be a shock from his appearance, long hair, muscular body, but it would be the tattoos, especially the one on his arm that would stun the most. His smile widened.

Two days ago, he had pulled into Lincolnville, Georgia. Riley had set him up in a two-room apartment at Anna's Boarding House on the east side, seven miles from the west side. The whole town comprised of less than fifteen thousand inhabitants.

As he passed what the locals called the strip mall, he almost laughed outright. No large chain stores as anchors. If you wanted a loaf of bread or a gallon of milk, you had only Lou's Grocery. If a hammer was your desire, no decision between Lowe's and Home Depot need be made, you wandered over to The Hardware Hutch. For a sit-down meal, you chose Fred's Diner, the local greasy spoon. The closest fast food was Betty's Bakery, where you'd grab a quick bite and a cup of coffee.

Today, Matthew rode over for breakfast at Fred's. The advertisement of blueberry pancakes on the window had caught his eye the day before.

He eased the bike into an open space near the entrance. When he slid his helmet off, his hair fell to the middle of his back. He climbed the steps and inhaled the balmy air. The double front doors had two signs. The left read "Open", the other "Please Use the Other Door". Matthew did as the sign instructed.

The smell of grease hit him like a frying pan to the skull. Smoke from the grill made the air heavy. The A/C did little to aid in dispersing the thickness as sweat drops burst onto his forehead. The backwash of noise faded to a murmur as he entered.

"You can sit where you like," a wrinkled-face man said.

Matthew nodded and took a step toward the back. Curious onlookers watched as he advanced.

Red vinyl stools lined the counter to his left. Booths swathed in the same red vinyl lined the opposite wall, reminding him of diners he'd seen in older television shows. He made his way through the narrow passage, giving a slight nod to those who met his glance. Most turned as he approached.

A table against the rear wall sat empty, making him feel more at ease. Something he brought with him from his undercover days. The farthest seat was the best vantage point—you could catch trouble as it entered, usually through the front.

In his printed t-shirt and faded jeans, he felt out of place compared to the neatly dressed patrons. When he removed his coat before sliding in, the whispering started. He knew the top portion of the snake tattoo was visible on his neck.

"Coffee, sir?" A petite server stopped beside the table. She'd tucked her brunette hair into a bun on the top of her head. The red apron surrounding her waist showed signs of a busy morning. Her nametag read Dolly.

"I'd prefer a glass of orange juice and a stack of those blueberry pancakes you have advertised, Dolly." He pointed to the large block letters on the window.

"I'll bring that right out to you." She quickly retreated.

Matthew continued to scan the patrons. Most wrenched their necks, trying not to appear obvious with their stares. All except one woman. He wasn't sure if he considered her appealing because of her looks or because she returned his gaze. He gauged her to be in her early thirties and her mood as troubled, if the frown and dark circles under the blue-purple eyes were any indication. Even with the shadows encircling the almond-shaped eyes, she captivated him. He had to fight to pull his attention from her.

As he waited for his food, he observed kids stuffing pancakes into their mouths faster almost than they got them on their fork. A hint of how good they might taste, he hoped.

Families filled most of the booths. Older men with a scattering of older women sat on the stools at the counter. The one thing they all had in common, the designer jeans they wore either in dark navy or black. There wasn't one faded, oversized pair among the group. You wouldn't chance upon anyone with their backsides hanging out in this crowd. Even the teenagers seemed well-fitted. Matthew hoped he hadn't fallen into some sort of Stepford society where all the children were perfect.

Dolly returned with five pancakes and a tray that held jars of strawberry and grape jam and a bottle of maple syrup. Matthew glanced over the jellies but chose syrup for his topping. He paused after his first bite. The food proved as tasty as the gulping children indicated.

After finishing his breakfast, he stood to leave. The smell of flowers swept over him. He stopped, taking in the aroma.

"Excuse me, please." A feminine voice with an irritated overtone sounded behind him.

Matthew twisted, coming face to face with the woman who had held his attention earlier. A lump rose in his throat, causing him to lose any other thoughts he might have had. He sized her up, noticing the rings on her left hand. For some unknown reason, disappointment flushed over him.

"Do you plan to stand there staring all day, or can I get through?" She placed a hand on her hip.

She knew the effect she had on a man. He tugged his jacket on, making her wait a moment longer than necessary because of the irritation he sensed from her attitude. It wasn't a very Christian thing to do, but God was still working on him with some things.

"Be my guest." He finally moved aside, allowing her through the double doors heading to the restroom area. Too bad most beautiful women had the ego to go with it. More than likely, she married the local football hero, and they were extremely happy.

Outside, the breeze had lessened, making the weather humid. The meteorologist had given a forecast of scattered showers. He'd kept his word thus far.

Once on the bike, Matthew glanced over his shoulder toward the window and saw people's heads spinning so he wouldn't be aware they'd been scrutinizing him. Everyone except her. The woman had returned to her seat and made no attempt to hide the fact she watched him. She unnerved him. He couldn't recall feeling as insecure as he did at that second. Her stare burned into him as he drove off.

He hoped she wouldn't be anywhere near for his first official day tomorrow. Her presence would only add to the anxiety he already felt.

GOOSE BUMPS REMAINED on Lydia's arms. The loud motorcycle caused everyone to take notice, but she by no means expected someone so attractive to step from it. Her pulse stopped when he walked through the door. His long hair didn't shock her, but she thought he'd have stubble covering his chin. However, the view alarmed her. His facial features, clean shaven, had the most ideal attributes she'd ever seen. Everything appeared flawless, from his pointed nose and raised cheekbones, right down to his full lips. She could only describe him as thoroughly gorgeous.

He sat in the rear, looking out over the crowd. Most patrons crooked their heads so fast when he glanced at them, it surprised her they didn't suffer whiplash. However, when it came to directing herself away, she couldn't. He had somehow captured her attention, and she discovered it hard to turn loose. If he hadn't broken away first, they'd likely still be staring at each other.

"Who do you suppose that was?" Warren Anniston jabbed his thumb toward the back table.

"I heard someone new was staying at Anna's." Sheryl Coufield blew into her coffee. "Maybe that's him. He's definitely nice to look at, isn't he?"

"With the leather jacket, it looks like he belonged in jail, not out here with decent people," Warren argued. "Did you notice that tattoo sticking out over his t-shirt?"

"It only added to his machismo," Sheryl said. "Even Lydia stared."

"It's because I'm not used to seeing men like that in Lincolnville." Lydia popped the last strawberry in her mouth. Of course, his penetrating blue eyes helped, she admitted to herself.

"I wonder who he's visiting. It'd be nice to take another peek before he leaves, like all the other single guys." Sheryl's lips formed a pout.

Lydia knew Sheryl's desire to have a family. She continually hunted for someone to be a good fit. The stranger appeared unlikely to be that special person she deserved. He was conceited with his loud ride that shouted, "Hey, everyone. Look at me!" And blocking the aisle, confirmed it more. It didn't bypass Lydia that he had taken his time putting on his coat before moving. The thought of shoving him aside brought a quick smile. She could almost hear the gasps from the other customers if she had.

"You've been awful quiet." Sheryl tossed a ten on the table to cover her share of the check.

"I'm tired. I received another call last night." Lydia prayed they would soon stop. "Warren and I are going shopping to find a system that'll block them."

The three met for breakfast every Saturday. Normally they would have eaten in Chattanooga, but this week was Warren's choice. Because Sheryl remarked a day or two earlier about him balding on top, and

Sheryl hated greasy food, Warren chose Fred's as a way of punishing her. It would have been a punishment for Lydia as well if it weren't for their fruit dish.

Of course, this morning, Fred's did offer the added floor show of the attractive man on the motorcycle.

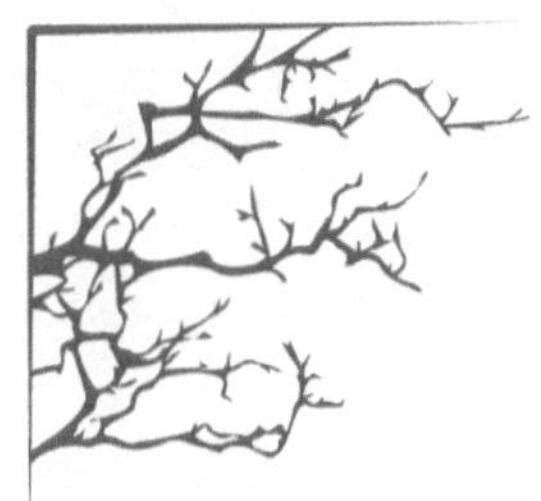

2

The rain had finally let up as Lydia maneuvered into a parking spot behind Warren's blue Ford Taurus sedan. She had deliberated not coming but forced herself from bed. It was even harder to convince herself to dress. What would it hurt if she missed one Sunday? Another call awakened her the night before, causing sleeplessness and a tear-stained pillow. The new telephone system hadn't worked yet to keep the intruder out.

Warren stepped from his car when she arrived. He wore a water-stained tan suit, yellow shirt, and in his right hand he carried a dark green umbrella. She knew he waited to escort her. He always did.

"You're running a bit late." He tightened the indigo tie stuffed under his neck. He combed his hair to the side to hide the balding Sheryl had mentioned days before.

Lydia clutched her Bible in her right hand and her Gucci purse in the other. "I received another call. The Caller ID gave some 800 number. When I dialed it back, a recording said it wasn't taking incoming calls."

"I'm sorry to hear that." Warren offered her his elbow, which she accepted. "I would have come over if you'd let me know. I was absorbed in a wonderful book and couldn't seem to put it down. I would have come over and stayed with you."

Both stopped as a loud roar sounded to their left. Lydia stared as an onyx and gold motorcycle from yesterday pulled into the lot. The noise from the bike caught anyone's attention within earshot. Lydia's heart bounced into her throat. How could the likes of this man like that excite her?

9

"You'd think we were starting a biker gang," Warren said.

"I hope he's here to be saved and not cause trouble." Lydia stifled a yawn. She gave a last glance toward the bike before proceeding toward the church for the ten o'clock service. "Have you heard anything about the new pastor?"

"No." Warren swerved to avoid a puddle. "Sheryl doesn't have any information either. The committee kept everything hush-hush. They're likely afraid if we discovered they picked some old geezer, nobody would show up."

"Finally." Sheryl pushed her thick blonde curls to the side as she greeted the two. "I wasn't sure you were going to make it. If I hadn't saved you a seat, you'd have to stand."

"It looks like all the neighboring towns have come out," Warren said.

Sheryl grabbed hold of Warren's other arm and dragged them to the second row. "I bet that's what the committee had in mind when they kept everything so quiet. People would come just to scrutinize who they chose."

"I hope it's not someone dull who'll put me to sleep." Warren shrugged off his jacket. "It'd be nice to have somebody who would wake up this sleepy town."

"Whoever he is, as long as God brought him here, he'll do fine." Lydia tried being the voice of reason, even though she wished the same thing. A fire and brimstone sermon would certainly keep her from dozing off.

Her parents had raised her in this old church. Grandfather had been its first preacher. It always made her feel secure whenever she walked in. After all these years, as she entered the sanctuary, the full beauty still captured her breath. Large chandeliers spread over each section of oak pillars, suspended from amber-colored wrought iron. The hand-blown glass florets had been specifically created for the worship area. The pulpit sat on a raised stage below a large arch. Above the podium hung a wooden cross Lydia's father brought home from Jerusalem and presented as a gift to the congregation.

However, lately, church had lost its luster for Lydia. She wondered if it was because her husband no longer sat beside her. She fought a tear slipping from her eye.

"Are you okay?" Sheryl's hand on hers stirred Lydia from her painful memories.

"A memory of Justin rushed in."

"Why are we in the second pew?" Warren interrupted. "You must have found out he's single and wanted a closer view."

"That's not why. I'm making sure we can hear everything clearly. That's all." Sheryl shook from anticipation. "Did you say he was single?"

Warren and Lydia chuckled.

Lydia glanced through the crowd, waving as others looked her way. Not since Justin's funeral had such a crowd gathered. As that thought rushed over her, she wished she had stayed in bed. She had gone through her wedding album after the caller had awakened her. It only depressed her more.

James Newman, III, one of the church deacons, walked to the pulpit and said a quick prayer. Lydia sensed anger from the darkness in his eyes. Could he be that upset about the committee's choice? Being a city councilman, he thought he could get what he wanted.

After two songs from the praise and worship group, James returned to the stage.

"Ladies and gentlemen." He leaned into the microphone at the lectern. His white hair was more pronounced because of the dark suit he wore. "We spent a great deal of time trying to find the best person to lead our flock. I hope he meets with your approval. The committee chose to go with someone younger. After all, it's the next generation that will be in charge of our community soon." James shifted from one foot to the other.

"I hear the choice made him mad," Sheryl whispered. "He had nominated Old Man Nesmith, and the committee said they wanted an outsider. They figured some new blood might attract younger couples from the surrounding towns."

"Probably why he wore black." Warren added. "If I didn't know any better, I'd say he was in mourning."

"Without further delay," James continued, "please welcome Matthew Winters."

The clapping slowed as Matthew took the stage. Jaws dropped throughout the room. Even Lydia's mouth hung wide as the motorcyclist strolled to the podium. His long, brown hair, pulled back, fell below his shoulders. A deep blue shirt was partially hidden under a black leather jacket. A dark pair of jeans led to ebony pointed cowboy boots. Below the left side of his firm jaw sat the tattoo of a snake ready to strike. His tall frame and broad shoulders reeked of masculinity, even with the ponytail.

"The committee has lost its mind." Warren spoke loud enough to cause a snicker in the crowd.

A warm smile appeared on the stranger's face, softening his features. Lydia's pulse beat faster. Who could blame her? God designed great masterpieces.

"Give him a chance. You could actually like him." Sheryl sat straighter in the pew. "Besides, he's good looking. And if I'm not mistaken, there's not a wedding band." She practically sang the last part.

The minister's gaze skimmed the crowd. Lydia became aware his focus rested on her. She could feel her body warm as she forced her breathing to stay even. He must have recalled their encounter at the diner. She wasn't exactly friendly, but then, neither was he. Those sapphire blues made her feel he could gaze into her inner core and see every emotion she experienced. After giving attention to a wrinkle in her skirt, she was able to compose herself. She hoped the heat that had rushed through her remained hidden from the others.

He preached for less than an hour on a topic she believed he chose carefully—not judging a book by its cover. His sermon contained humorous anecdotes, along with a serious message. While he spoke, no one left their seat. The entire congregation seemed to enjoy him. Everyone but James Newman, III, whose jaw clenched throughout the entire service. With every "Amen" from the crowd, his teeth tightened. Lydia thought she heard them grinding from the other side of the aisle.

"I swear James is about to have a heart attack," Warren whispered once the sermon was complete. "From how red his face is, I think he's going to explode."

"James isn't used to being told no," Lydia said. "But he'll adjust. He always does."

Matthew Winters wound his way to the doorway to greet parishioners as they left. Six-foot-three or four, and powerfully built, his jeans gave a hint as to his masculine legs and bottom. Lydia jerked her head away to keep from staring. No matter how nice, it had to be disrespectful to stare at a minister like that, particularly in a church. Her grandfather's church at that. Praying for forgiveness, she grabbed her purse from the pew.

"Lydia, my dear." James tugged her into a hug. "How are you today?"

"I'm doing well. How are you and Melanie?" Garlic emanated from his breath. She ran her hand discreetly across her nose.

"We're fine." James shook hands with Warren and pecked Sheryl's cheek. "What did you three think of Mr. Winters?"

"I liked him. I believe he'll do wonderful," Warren said with more enthusiasm than he should have. "On the other hand, Sheryl considers him dreamy."

"Very funny, Warren." Sheryl nudged him with her elbow.

"She apparently isn't alone." James flashed a glance in Matthew's direction at the back of the sanctuary.

Three single women giggled around him. A wave of jealousy crossed over Lydia, taking her by surprise.

"I suggest you hurry. The masses are already gathering." Warren poked Sheryl in the ribs.

"Lydia, how about you drop by for lunch?" James held Lydia by the wrist. "Melanie would love to visit with you, and Jimmy will be there. He's fresh out of another rehab stint and could use a friend."

"Unfortunately, we already have plans." Sheryl chimed in. "How long will he be staying with you?"

"I'm not positive. Hopefully long enough to pull himself together." James released his hold. "Maybe some other time." He nodded before making his retreat.

A sigh of relief came over Lydia. "I don't recall making any plans. What are we doing?"

"Anything to keep James from trying to fix you up with his loser son." Sheryl rolled her eyes. "Let's get in line and introduce ourselves to the new minister."

"You two go ahead. I want to go over and talk to Wendy," Warren said. "Besides, I'd hate to find myself caught in the swarm of women who are about to devour the new preacher."

Sheryl kept her eyes on Warren as he walked to the stage where Wendy Moreland gathered sheet music. "Do you think he likes her?"

"If he does, I hope it's reciprocated," Lydia said. "Wendy's a nice lady. They'd make a good couple."

"Let's meet the new minister." Sheryl dragged Lydia forward. "It'll be hard concentrating with a preacher who's so *hot*. But it's a sacrifice I'm willing to make."

"I'm tired. I'm just going to head home." Lydia wanted to slink far from this man. Just a day before she yearned to smack him for blocking her route at Fred's Diner.

"Not before greeting Matthew. I like that name. It's so biblical." Sheryl caught Lydia by the arm. "Besides, your grandparents are founding members, so you need to welcome him. It's proper protocol."

"If he was seventy and ugly, would it still be proper?" Lydia grudgingly went along. As she proceeded forward, a shudder came over, as if being spied on.

"What's wrong?" Sheryl leaned into her. "I could tell you barely heard half of what was preached. Is it Justin?"

"No. Well, a little." Lydia motioned for Sheryl to pull out of line and go to the far end of a pew for privacy. "I'm still receiving the calls, even after buying the new phone."

"Can you tell who it is yet?"

"No. It sounds like they're disguising their voice."

"It has to be somebody you would recognize, otherwise why change their voice?"

"That's the worst part." Lydia scoured the sanctuary, glancing at those she used to trust. "It could be anyone." She hesitated before continuing. "He doesn't say much except he's watching me. And I swear he's..." Lydia hoped to make Sheryl understand without having to say it.

"He's what?"

"You know." Lydia nodded her head at an angle and raised her eyebrows to get her friend to understand.

"You mean he's—" Sheryl's tone raised an octave, causing people to turn in their direction. "That's sick."

They stood in silence, waiting for the others to return to their own business.

"Let's do lunch at your house," Sheryl said. "We'll bring Warren, too. Whoever it is won't mess with you as long as he's with us." She referred to Warren's six-foot build. He'd taken up weightlifting and boxing in the past year and gone from a scrawny man to a muscular one.

"He only calls at night. I'm certain it's to make me fully aware of him." Lydia skimmed the faces of the stragglers in the sanctuary as though she might see some hint as to her irritant. "If that's their plan, it's working."

"We should make Riley aware of what's happening."

"The police have been over, but they can't trace the caller. I'm not sure it's something to worry the sheriff about."

"It can't be a coincidence. The anniversary of Justin's death is in a couple of days, and you start getting anonymous calls. It doesn't sound right." Sheryl leaned in closer as a deacon passed by. "We'll stop by really quick and say hi to the pastor as we leave."

Lydia straggled behind. The closer they got to Matthew, the more anxious she became. She knew it would be silly to hope he didn't recall her.

"Pastor, it's a pleasure to meet you. My name is Sheryl Coufield." She gushed. "This is my friend Lydia Frederickson."

Lightning shot up Lydia's arm as masculine fingers covered her hand. She gathered all her power not to yank away. His eyes caused a skip in her heartbeat as she stared into their rich blue color, similar to a clear pool any woman would long to dive into.

"Lydia, that's an enchanting name." He continued his hold. "Were you named for the woman in the book of Acts?"

She nodded, unable to speak. Her mouth seemed glued shut. She hoped nobody else detected the beads of sweat popping out on her forehead.

"We bumped into each other, almost literally, yesterday." He paused before adding, "At the diner."

The heat from a blush ran over her face and down her neck. She got the impression he enjoyed her discomfort, proving her assessment of him the day before had been on target.

"And how did you ladies like my sermon?"

"It was all right." Lydia decided against announcing she thought him arrogant. He had stood over the parishioners like a Pharisee. He'd known his long hair and tattoos would be a shock to the congregation.

What bothered her more was the smug look he currently wore. Her eagerness to slap it off his face grew. How awful. She'd barely met the guy and twice had been inclined to knock him about.

James reached over Lydia, brushing her shoulder, and extended his hand toward Matthew. The touch unexpectedly disturbed her.

"We'll see you next week." Lydia shuddered as she raced to the parking lot, hoping fresh air would help.

"I can't believe you did that." Sheryl panted, following quickly on her heels. "Shrugging off the new minister like that was rude. I don't recall ever seeing you act like this before."

"I'm sorry. The more I contemplated what you said, the more nervous I became." She hoped she hid the frenzy in her mind. The recent events had begun to color how she viewed people she once believed were friends. "I'm positive the person calling me is someone I know."

MATTHEW STOOD IN THE sanctuary doorway as he remembered the silence when he first took the podium. A smile came over his lips upon recalling the shocked expressions of the congregation. His heart had stood in his throat as he scrutinized the astonished sea of people, only to be stopped dead in his tracks by the woman from the diner. The lady had mesmerizing eyes, a soft blue-violet. She had an appearance that could hold a man's attention for days. Seldom did his mind wander, but he needed every ounce of energy to turn and regain his composure.

He glanced at this dazzling woman a bit later, but it was obvious she'd tuned him out. Why bother attending if you're going to ignore the Word? He imagined she only came to impress others in this rural area.

When she approached him, as she was leaving, her perfume drifted over him, strong yet soft. Something told him she could be the same. He pictured himself a cartoon character who floated in the air behind her, mesmerized by the whiff of a pretty girl. When they touched, a tremor ran through his body. It was the same sensation as when he was a small child and had stuck a wet finger into a light socket. He could have sworn contact with Lydia Frederickson curled his hair.

Her eyes stared through him as if taking every secret he'd ever had from their dark hiding places. The thought caused him unease. Not that he had any secrets, just sins in his past he'd buried long ago.

When she spoke, the smoky tone of her voice pulled at him, and the only words he could muster were about seeing her in the diner. The blush that came over her told him there was discomfort with his words, though he couldn't understand why. However, when James Newman, III reached around her, fear flashed in her eyes. Matthew had an urge to protect her from Newman's touch as she ran to her car. He was positive she wiped at her cheeks as she rushed out. Anger rose inside at the thought of her crying. It was a feeling he had to shake in order to get his jaw to loosen.

He strolled through the double-hung doors. This was *his* sanctuary. At least until the ninety-day trial period was over. Its beauty surprised him the first day, with its oak pews and deep blue upholstered cushions. The richness of the wood yelled class. At the rear of the stage sat two rows of chairs for the praise and worship team. Candelabras stood at the sides of the stage, each holding six large, tapered candles.

"What are you thinking on so intently?" Riley Owens came up behind.

"Recalling my first day," Matthew said. "I looked for you this morning."

A holster on Riley's hip held a .9-mm Beretta. Over his heart, attached to the tan Lincolnville Sheriff's Office uniform, hung a silver sheriff's badge.

"Unfortunately, duty calls, even on Sundays," Riley said.

"I enjoy having regular days off." Matthew replaced a Bible in the slot of a pew.

"I'll bet. Of course, if you discover this job doesn't work out, I still have room for you." Riley sat in the front pew. "So, how'd your first day go? Did you astonish them all?"

"Probably more amazed I didn't rob them."

"I imagine. Some guy who looks like a thug turning out to be a preacher." Riley raised the left side of his mouth into a small grin, the closest Matthew had ever seen to a smile. "But by the end, you had them mesmerized and shouting "Amen's" to the ceiling."

"I'm not so sure about that, but overall, I'd say it went very well." Matthew enjoyed preaching. It gave him elation unlike any job he'd known. "So, what are your plans for today?" He sat down next to Riley.

"I have to visit someone having a problem. In fact, she's a member of your congregation. Seems prank calls have been wrecking her sleep." Riley hesitated, a distant look in his eye. "They have her pretty upset."

"You actually go in person for that." Matthew knew in a big city most officers took a report over the phone, filed it, and hoped nothing tragic befell the victim.

"That's life in a small town. Besides, her husband was a close friend of mine." Riley's black cowboy hat swung from hand to hand as he leaned forward. "He's the reason I took this job. I told him I'd watch out for her when he died."

Matthew caught his friend's pained expression. Whenever he dealt with this woman, memories of Riley's own loss had to crawl back up to the surface. "I'm sorry about your friend. It sounds like you were close."

Riley nodded. "He had cancer and lingered quite a while." Riley leaned back. He shook his head as if trying to get something out. "Maybe you'd like to come."

"Why should I do that?"

"She's a parishioner, and her husband died two years ago this week." Riley stared at the cross. "Maybe more psychological than real. The death hit her pretty hard."

"I imagine." Matthew got to his feet. "I'll agree, but only if you come for dinner at Brenda's. If you go, I can at least make a case for not being married when you're not either."

"Your sister still giving every effort to pinpoint that special person for you?"

"More than special. A wife." Matthew flipped off the church lights. The two of them walked out, and he locked the outer doors to the building.

"Tired of you being a bachelor?" Riley opened his car door. "You better be careful. She probably has a few candidates in mind."

Matthew nodded. "That's what I'm afraid of."

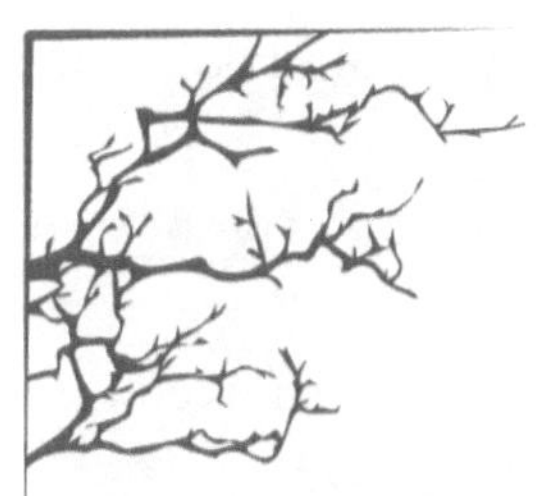

3

"This is ridiculous." Lydia threw the eggshell in the disposal. "What can Riley do about the prank calls?" Having to describe the incident gave her a knot in her stomach.

"I believe it warrants him stopping by." Sheryl gave a firm nod. "He'd want to know, especially with how upset it made you this morning."

"I think it's an excuse so you can see him," Warren said. "I'm not sure it's for Lydia's benefit or your own."

"I have absolutely no interest in Riley Owens. Just because he's one of the few single men in Lincolnville doesn't mean a thing." Sheryl added slyly. "Besides, there's a new man in town. And he's single, too."

"You sound like a desperate teenager waiting for a boy to ask you to the prom." Warren grinned.

"Stop it, you two, or I'll have to separate you." It amazed Lydia how Sheryl and Warren kidded each other constantly, like a pair of squabbling young siblings. Having known each other since grade school, they were as close as any family she knew.

"And exactly how's your love life?" Sheryl teased Warren. "I haven't seen you out lately, though you seemed rather cozy with Wendy Moreland this morning. Do you plan to ask her out?"

"Probably not."

"Why?" Lydia said. "She's a nice lady."

"There isn't that type of attraction, that spark," Warren said.

Heat rose in Lydia as she remembered the voltage from Matthew's touch. His shocked look told her he felt it too. It must have been static electricity. She would never be attracted to someone so egotistical.

21

Sure, he was handsome, but most men with that type of look had the attitude to go with it.

"There isn't always a spark," Sheryl said. "Sometimes you need to make your own electricity."

"This coming from the world's oldest virgin." Warren smirked.

Sheryl slugged him in the shoulder, causing him to wince.

A knock sounded at the door.

"I got it." Sheryl sprang from the stool at the sound of a knock at the door. "That should be Riley." Before opening the door, she whispered, "And look who's with him—the new pastor."

"Great," Lydia said. She hoped the earlier spark had been a solitary thing.

"You be nice." Sheryl let out a giggle. "You could do worse than a preacher for a husband."

"I already had a husband." Guilt swept over Lydia as she thought of another man in the house she shared with Justin.

Sheryl guided Riley and Matthew into the living-room. Warren brought cups from the kitchen while Lydia carried the coffee.

"Riley, it's wonderful of you to come by." Lydia placed the silver carafe on the coffee table. "I probably shouldn't have bothered you with this, but Sheryl insisted."

"We all know how determined she can be." Riley gave Lydia a kiss on her cheek.

"Pastor Winters, nice to meet you again." She gritted her teeth, hoping the current she'd felt earlier had faded. A wish not granted.

"Matthew and I have known each other for a while," Riley said. "I brought him, because as your minister, he may well be of some service."

"In case it turns out I'm a crazy widow lady with a vivid imagination. The only thing missing is a houseful of cats." Lydia retreated to a nearby wall.

"That's not what I meant by inviting him." Riley stared at the ground.

"I notice you didn't argue my sanity." Her laughter sounded empty even to her. "I'm not a fool Riley. It's been two years since Justin died. Either the calls are a coincidence, or I'm losing my mind. Maybe the preacher here can do an exorcism to release all my inner demons." She waved her hands as she spoke.

"Lydia!" Sheryl's voice had a harsh tone.

Lydia inhaled a deep breath, then motioned for the visitors to sit.

"Maybe it's not such a coincidence." Matthew finally spoke. "There might be something to the fact the calls are coming at this particular time?"

"What do you mean?" Lydia's insides shook.

"If the caller lives nearby, they have to be familiar with your husband's death. Calling now would make it even more distressing." Matthew stirred sugar into his cup. "If it's kids, they'd do it as a prank to scare you not to bring sorrow."

"I can't bear that thought." Lydia forced herself to look away from Matthew's tanned skin and his perfect lips. Why was she thinking about his lips? Maybe she was crazy.

"What thought?" Sheryl's eyes held concern.

"The calls are coming because of the anniversary of Justin's death. That would mean they're doing it to hurt me." The battle of the tears lost, she darted into the kitchen.

Riley followed her. "What's going on? This is about more than just the phone calls. What is it?"

"I don't know what's wrong with me."

Riley pulled her into a hug as her silent tears became sobs.

MATTHEW REMAINED WITH Warren and Sheryl. When Riley suggested he come along, he hadn't considered the widow would be the brunette whose eyes distracted him while giving his sermon. As silence fell over the room, Matthew scanned the space, taking in the soft yellow on the walls. The tan floorboards added a pleasant contrast. The plush chairs where Sheryl and Warren sat matched the multi-colors of the sofa he was on. Beside Matthew stood a walnut end table where a display of symbols lay atop a folder.

"That's Lydia's work," Sheryl said. "She creates logos for websites. It takes plenty of talent and quite an imagination."

Matthew picked up a slip of paper with a pencil drawing. It was a pair of hands placed over a keyboard, the logo for a typing service. Simple, yet effective. "I always wondered how companies got their logos."

"For larger companies, it's probably done in-house or by an advertising firm. Smaller companies don't have the resources, so they hire Lydia to do it for them."

Matthew replaced the document on top of the file folder. The photograph of a younger man stared from a black picture frame. Her late husband, he assumed. His dark features would have been a great fit for Lydia. They must have made a striking couple.

Feeling restless, he rose from the sofa, glancing at photos standing in frames over the red brick fireplace. Happier times. Her husband appeared to be in his late twenties, his features fading from cancer.

"She really misses him." Sheryl followed and picked up a framed photograph from the mantel. "She hasn't changed one thing about this house since he died."

"Maybe she's afraid if she did it would erase him even more." Sorrow filled Matthew as he contemplated the pain Lydia must have suffered.

Sheryl brushed aside her thick hair. Distress filled her light blue eyes as she glanced toward the kitchen.

Matthew continued to scan the pictures. His stomach jumped at a photograph at the end. Lydia posed with a dark-haired boy in his mid-teens. The recognition was instant. Charlie Westerman.

He flashed to a horrible scene before he'd become a minister, while still in the Drug Enforcement Agency. They'd arranged a sting operation that went wrong. He could still see a young woman kneeling beside Charlie's lifeless body. Her voice still haunted him.

"He just wanted a cigarette. Why'd you kill him?" The woman dressed in blue jeans and a black leather vest sobbed.

Sheryl's voice brought Matthew back to the present. "That was Lydia's brother. He died in Miami." Sheryl shook her head. "She's lost so much too soon. Barely thirty and two people she was close to gone."

Matthew couldn't take his eyes off the picture. His pulse drowned out any further conversation with Sheryl. "Excuse me, please." Matthew had to get out of there before he lost all composure.

As he walked toward the kitchen, he could hear Lydia's voice breaking. "I wonder if it'll ever be easier."

"I'm certain it will," Riley said. "Someday you'll look up and have only happy memories."

Matthew entered the room. Unexpected jealousy rushed through him when he saw Riley holding Lydia in his arms. He cleared his throat. "Excuse me. I didn't mean to interrupt. Is there anything I can do to help?"

"There's nothing that can be done at this moment." Riley released Lydia. "Not until this guy makes his next move."

"I'm not talking about the caller. As your minister, if you need to pray or talk, my door is always open." Matthew laid a hand on her shoulder.

"Thank you." Lydia wiped her eyes with a tissue.

"We'll have a car drive by sporadically, in case someone's watching you." Riley told her.

"I appreciate that." Lydia leaned against his shoulder as she led them out. "Thanks for everything."

As they sat in the drive, Riley pounded his palm on the steering wheel. "She hasn't had much happiness in the last few years. Watching Justin die all but shut her down. When he passed, his mom was so upset, she moved in for Lydia to take care of her. She died about eight months ago, allowing Lydia to finally grieve. She was actually coming out of it."

Matthew's pulse continued to beat in his ears. What are the chances he'd come into a town where Charlie's family lived? He needed to focus on other things. "What type of cancer did her husband have?"

"Prostate. They found out weeks after their wedding. It doesn't seem fair. That house holds her hostage with all her memories. It's frozen in time with the same pictures and Justin's items lying around since his death." Riley paused. "And all her pain. She only leaves to go to church and volunteer work in Chattanooga."

"You sound as if you care deeply for her." Matthew wished Riley would put the car in gear.

"Justin and I were close, closer than some brothers. I sure hope we can figure out who's doing this. The anniversary of Justin's death is coming, and we always visit the gravesite. I'm worried she'll fall apart completely if these calls continue."

Matthew nodded, more concerned with how she'd react once she discovered her minister was the man who killed her brother.

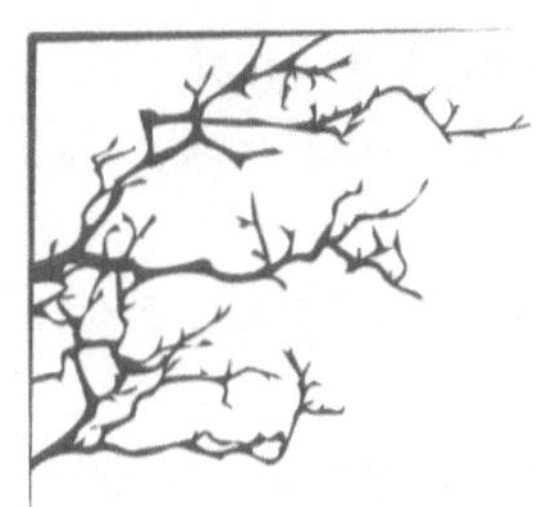

4

Lydia wiped her cheek as she cleaned the coffee mugs in the sink.

"I'm worried about you." Sheryl brought in the carafe.

"I'll be fine." Lydia brushed at another tear. "I can't seem to quit crying these days."

"You seem so quiet. I have a feeling it's more than the timing of these calls."

"What do you mean?"

"You were just short of rude to the pastor. That's twice in the same day. What's up?" Sheryl emptied the coffee into the sink. "Blaming Justin isn't going to work."

"I hadn't realized running out so a stranger couldn't watch me fall apart was rude." Lydia threw the dishtowel on the counter. "Maybe I am losing my mind."

"Sheryl is just wondering if you have your eye on the new pastor, so you'll take your paws off Riley," Warren said as he came in.

"Off Riley?" Lydia smiled. "We're only friends."

"I know that." Sheryl aimed daggers at Warren.

Lydia grinned at the prospect of Riley and Sheryl together as a couple. As much as she cared for Sheryl, she could be a bit of a drama queen while Riley was totally serious.

"You would make a wonderful pair, the town sheriff and the town gossip." Warren slid his arm over Sheryl's shoulder. "He would save money not having to pay an informant ever again."

Sheryl jabbed him in the ribs with her elbow.

"Well, ladies, I must bid you a fond farewell. Unlike Sheryl, I, myself, have a life." Warren gave Lydia a light kiss, catching her ear. "I'll stay if you wish."

"That won't be necessary. I'm planning to take a nap." Lydia patted his arm. "You go do what you have to."

She walked Warren to the door, her eyes heavy from lack of sleep. Sheryl had taken a seat on the sofa.

"You don't have to stay," Lydia said.

"I know, but you need rest." Sheryl dug through her purse while she spoke, pulling out a hardcover book. "Go. I'll answer the phone and later we can do dinner."

Lydia dozed for a couple of hours. When she returned downstairs, Sheryl was in the same spot on the couch. They chatted while fixing dinner. Lydia had a hard time focusing on anything but Matthew's touch.

"I guess I should be leaving so you can get some more sleep." Sheryl replaced the placemats on the table after the meal.

"You mean rest until my caller contacts me again?"

"If they're watching you, they're aware the sheriff has been here, so that could deter them." Sheryl reasoned. "Besides, if it's a kid, they'll be in school tomorrow, so they won't be up that late."

"I hope so."

"Maybe if you get some sleep, at Wednesday night's service, you can actually be civil to Matthew."

"Did I really treat him that badly?"

"For anyone else, maybe not. But for you, yes."

"I guess I'll apologize when I bump into him next. I'm out of sorts right now." Being distant to Matthew had more to do with Matthew than with the calls. She found herself drawn to him in a way she hadn't been to a man in a long time.

"He appears to be nice and will understand," Sheryl said. "But if I were you, I'd be careful."

"Careful of what?"

"I swear I saw a glint of lust when he looked at you." Sheryl grinned.

"It's hard to imagine a minister having lustful thoughts of me, or anyone else for that matter." Heat ran across Lydia's cheeks.

"Well, I'll be. You're blushing." Sheryl touched Lydia's arm. "You find him attractive. Don't you?"

"He is nice looking, so what?" Lydia shrugged her shoulders while her insides did hurdles.

"Nothing. It's great you find him attractive. It proves you're alive."

"But there's too much overconfidence in his attitude. The only reason there's an attraction is because of his looks." Lydia played with the frayed edges of a cloth placemat. "I prefer a person who has some substance on the inside."

"When a person looks that good, who needs substance?" Sheryl giggled. "Imagine him holding you at night. He could be hollow for all I care."

"You know that's not true. You want someone who has more than just looks."

"Being handsome helps you forget some of the ego department. Besides, I can't recall any sign of conceit from Matthew. He's been quite nice to me. Maybe some of that haughtiness comes from how you've behaved."

"What do you mean?"

"You ran out on him at the church and here," Sheryl said. "That's not exactly saying friendly."

"Maybe I have been rude. It's been a hard couple of days." Lydia sighed. "I cared so much for Justin. How can I even look at somebody else?"

"It's been two years. It's not good for you to continue living with a memory." Sheryl grabbed Lydia's hand. "Justin wouldn't want you to sit here crying. He'd want you to be happy."

Emptiness filled her. "I'm not sure I can."

"Justin had Riley visiting quite a bit near the end. He might have hoped you two would hit it off. Maybe find comfort in each other's arms, so to speak. That obviously isn't going to happen, so maybe God put Matthew here for you instead."

"I doubt it. I can't believe I'll ever love that deeply again."

THE RINGING TELEPHONE pulled Lydia from a sound sleep. She glanced at the clock. The time was just shy of three o'clock in the morning. She hesitated to answer. Could it be the caller? What if something happened to one of her parents, and she didn't pick up?

"Hello." Her groggy voice answered.

"The yearnings are getting strong to touch you, to taste you."

"Stop calling! My husband died two years ago, and these calls are really upsetting me."

"It won't be too long until you're not alone anymore. I can't wait to feel you beneath..."

Lydia slammed the receiver down. She clicked on the nearby light and grabbed Justin's pillow and pulled it against her. If it had been a teenager harassing her, he would have hung up. Wouldn't he? A bead of sweat trickled from her forehead.

A few moments passed before a noise at the front door startled her. She grabbed her cell from the nightstand and crept to the top of the stairs. A shadowy figure appeared through the tapered glass on her door. Her fingers trembled as she pressed numbers on the telephone.

A knock sounded, followed by a man's harsh whisper. "Lydia, it's me. Riley."

The trembling in her stomach dissipated. She descended the stairs and threw open the door. She had never been happier to see that tan uniform.

"I happened to be passing by and saw your light come on. I wanted to check on you."

"He called again. He said awful things." She fought the frantic emotion climbing through her being. "Why is he doing this? Why now?"

MATTHEW DROVE INTO Lincolnville in the early morning hours. He should have followed Riley out when he left Brenda's. But when his nephew asked Matthew to stay to play a new video game, he couldn't resist. It was now almost three, and he had an early morning meeting.

Unlike a big city, no lights from local businesses lit his journey. The streets were dark except for the occasional streetlamp. For some inexplicable reason, he spun onto Devonshire Lane, the street where Lydia lived. As he rounded the corner, he tried to convince himself checking on a parishioner was part of his duty. Besides, monitoring Charlie's sister was the least he could do for the kid he'd killed. He could live with the excuses. It would be easier than admitting something about this woman had gotten under his skin.

He drove around the curve leading to the two-story white house. A Lincolnville Sheriff's Department cruiser was parked out front. He prayed nothing had happened. As he passed, he realized no lights shone in the house. His heart tumbled inside his chest. Even though Riley denied it, this proved they were involved. At first, it was the appearance of a friend comforting another friend. However, Riley spending the night left little doubt they were more.

Matthew sped off. At least with the sheriff there, Lydia would be safe. Matthew couldn't explain why, but a yearning grew inside that made him wish he'd been the man chosen to protect her.

His sleep was restless, so the next morning he rose early and drove around the area before heading to work. Fall colors littered his route. The maples had begun to change, scattering red and yellow throughout. He made a point of avoiding Devonshire during his ride. Riley stood beside the sheriff's cruiser in the church parking lot when Matthew pulled in. He parked next to the tan vehicle with a large silver seal and the words Lincolnville Sheriff emblazoned on the driver's side.

Matthew had no intention of mentioning he saw the car parked at Lydia's. With any luck, Riley had been asleep, and unaware Matthew drove by. Riley may have had an excuse for being at Lydia's. Matthew would have to fumble to think of one. "Riley, how are you this beautiful fall day?"

"Tired. Lydia received another call last night." Riley followed him into the building. "Can you spare a minute?"

"Sure."

No one would be to work for another half hour. Matthew flipped on overhead lights as they walked back to his office.

Riley carried his hat in his hand. Once in the office, he wandered to the large picture window. His face was drawn, and dark circles hung under his eyes. His whole façade gave the impression a dark cloud hung over his head.

"We can't seem to get a handle on the person making these calls," Riley said. "He's starting to say some pretty bad stuff."

Matthew sat back and listened, letting Riley speak without interruption.

"I heard your bike early, not too long after the call." Riley's voice lowered as he moved from the window to a seat across from Matthew. "Lydia's a bit out of your beaten path. Isn't she?"

Heat rose on Matthew's neck and onto his face as he worked on an explanation. Wouldn't do to say he found her attractive and just seeing her house excited him. Thankfully, Riley continued without waiting for a response.

"Did you note anything suspicious?"

"No. There wasn't anything out of the ordinary." The timing of his passing by soon after the phone call had to look funny. His defenses rose. "Is that why you suggested this job?" Matthew's tone sharpened. "In case you weren't aware of it, I'm here as a minister, not a personal bodyguard for your girlfriend."

"My girlfriend? Is that what you think? You drive by in the late-night hours, my car's parked out front, and you assume I'm sleeping with her. Not that it's any of your business, but I'm a friend to her. Nothing more. I happened to be reclined in the driver's seat of my car when you rode by."

Matthew's heart did a flip hearing there was no romantic liaison between the two. "Sorry. I shouldn't have jumped to any conclusions." He rounded the desk and slid a hip onto the edge.

"You were checking up on her?" Riley asked.

"Honestly, I still haven't quite figured out what I was doing."

"People wonder why I keep out of relationships." Riley gave his head a shake. "It's too much trouble, particularly in the emotion department. Look at you, acting as if you're afraid another guy's stealing your girl. Last I checked, she wasn't even close to being yours."

Matthew let out a laugh.

"Lydia's a wonderful lady," Riley said. "She's been remote since her husband died, but under that aloof exterior is a warm, caring person. I don't have a problem if it turned out to be you that got through to her, but be careful not to push too hard." He hesitated. "I feel bad for the gossip that's going to run rampant. If you believed we were together, others will too. It's just more for her to deal with."

"I don't recall any lights being on in the neighborhood, so most shouldn't be aware of your being there. I certainly won't say a word."

"Maybe I'm too close to it all. I still remember the pain from my end. I can't imagine what Lydia's gone through." Riley stood and returned to the window. "I spent eighteen months watching a good friend die, his wife at his side every minute, emotionally dying alongside him. It would probably have been easier if he'd died quickly. I promised him I'd look after her. But how do you protect someone from a voice in the night?" Riley's forehead creased, and his eyes went downcast. "I can't stop being there for her because of a bunch of tongue-waggers. I gave my word to a close friend."

"You can't stop being her friend." Matthew walked over and placed his hand on Riley's shoulder. "She needs prayer and friendship. That's all any of us can do at this point. Hopefully, this person will get tired and not take it to the next level."

LYDIA LINGERED IN THE parking lot. Finally, she opened the car door, grumbling as she gathered the books in her arms. She was here; might as well get it over with. Besides, Riley made her promise to get out of the house.

She inhaled a bottomless amount of air before entering the building. "Hi, Phyllis."

The secretary held up an index finger while she spoke into the telephone. Phyllis and her husband were fixtures of the church, having worked there for nearly fifteen years. Her husband cared for the grounds while she worked in the office. When Lydia called earlier, Phyllis confided to her that women had been calling all morning with silly excuses to stop by and see the new minister. Lydia imagined Phyllis was about ready to pull her white hair out.

Lydia became aware of his presence even before she saw him. Nothing prepared her for the energy she experienced when they again met.

"Phyllis, could you..." Matthew stopped mid-sentence when their eyes met. "How are you today, Ms. Frederickson?"

"I'm doing fine. And you?" Lydia offered her best smile as books tumbled from her arms.

"Let me get those for you." He bent to the floor, scooping books as he went. "It was only an hour ago I found out the Pendleton Library upstairs was named for your family."

"Mainly for my mom. This was her church before my parents moved to Savannah a few years ago." Lydia followed him to the second floor. "In fact, the library was her dream. It's the closest thing to a public library Lincolnville has."

They entered the large room. Bookshelves lined two walls. The far wall held fiction, the other non-fiction.

"Terri Blackstock, Beverly Lewis, Rick Warren." Matthew read the names of the authors on some of the books as he set them on a table holding a flat panel television. "These will be of great use. Thank you, Ms. Frederickson."

"Please, it's Lydia."

"And I'm Matthew." He held his hand out to her.

An inferno rushed through her frame as his hand touched hers. Salty drops inched over her lashes. She darted to the lady's room in the outer hall. How could she have fallen apart like that? After she dabbed her cheeks, she ran water over her face. If the new minister didn't believe she was crazy before, this should leave little doubt. When she opened the door, Matthew was leaning on the opposite wall with a leg bent. The lower tip of a cowboy boot showed below his black slacks. He wore an anxious look on his face.

"Are you all right?" He led her back to the library.

"I'm sorry." She patted at her eyes. "I can't seem to control my emotions lately. Some days I feel I'm losing my mind."

"Another phone call last night?" He motioned for her to sit in a rolling chair.

She obliged. "It only reminds me I'm alone."

"You might be physically alone, but God is always with you." Matthew rose. "Let me get you some water."

He returned from the outer hallway holding a red cup. Matthew knelt in front of her. Her fingers trembled as his hand covered hers, helping her when she raised the drink to her lips.

"It's a hard time of year for me. Not sleeping well isn't helping." Lydia battled to contain her sobs while she spoke, but her words came out like broken hiccups.

"I imagine. Riley mentioned you received another call." He tugged a couple of tissues from a nearby box and handed it to her.

Lydia nodded. "I wish they would stop, at least until after Thursday."

"Thursday?" Matthew pulled up a brown cushioned ottoman and sat facing her, their knees barely touching.

"The anniversary of Justin's death. I could probably handle it during a different time of year." She couldn't comprehend why she felt the eagerness to explain.

"There's no guarantee of that. These calls are meant to upset you. It doesn't matter when they're occurring."

"The worst part is it's probably somebody I know, a friend." Icy claws crept up her spine. "How can someone do this to another person?"

"I can't explain why people do the things they do. I wish sometimes God would interfere with the actions of man." Matthew paused. "But whenever you reach out for Him, God is there for you. And so are your friends. I know you and I just met, but you can trust me, Lydia."

"I appreciate that." She let out a half laugh. "The funny part is we met after the calls started. You really are the only person I *can* trust."

MATTHEW RECALLED THE rush that went through him when he first saw Lydia standing in the outer office. It was a mixture of euphoria with anxiety. Once she realized he was the cop who shot her brother, hatred would fill those beautiful eyes.

As he approached, he realized without high heels she went to his shoulders. Again, her alluring perfume captivated him. The caricature of himself floating behind her once again bounced into his mind. Her emotional display a few days before told him she was more than an egotistical beauty queen. Inside lived a sensitive person who harbored deep feelings for the people she loved.

Upstairs, he listened as she talked, asking her questions, prodding her to continue. He could hear the mourning and loss with each word. The tremor in her tone and the shakiness of her hands showed the depths of her pain. He spent over an hour listening to her convey her story of her husband's life and his death. When she had finished, tranquility came over her face.

When they returned to the lower floor, he realized he wanted more time with her. He longed to hear about her life, not only her husband, but everything, including her relationship with her brother. Had they been close when he died? Was she aware of the circumstances of his death? A force gathered in him to know all there was.

"I came by to drop off the books and for another reason as well," she said. "I hope you can forgive me for the way I acted the other day."

"I'm not sure what you mean." Matthew worked to erase the image of himself drifting helplessly behind that wonderful scent.

"I behaved badly after the service, and at my home. I was rude with how I treated you, and I'm sorry."

He placed a hand over his heart when it fluttered as he looked in her eyes. "First, I don't recall you acting badly at all. Second, you have more on your mind at the moment than fawning over some new stranger." Matthew gave her a grin, hoping the levity would make her mood improve.

"Matthew," Phyllis interrupted. "James Newman is on line two. This is the third call since you went upstairs. He's calling about his son."

"I'll be there after I walk Ms. Frederickson to her car. Duty calls." Matthew handed Lydia a business card. "Feel free to call anytime of the day or night."

"Thanks, I will." She waved to Phyllis before walking out the front double-hung doors with him.

Once back inside, Matthew watched as Lydia drove from the parking lot. There was something fascinating, yet remote about her.

"Excuse me." Phyllis hollered as Matthew continued to stare out the side window. "She's a very pretty lady, but if you keep Mr. Newman holding on any longer, you may find yourself officiating at his funeral before the week is out."

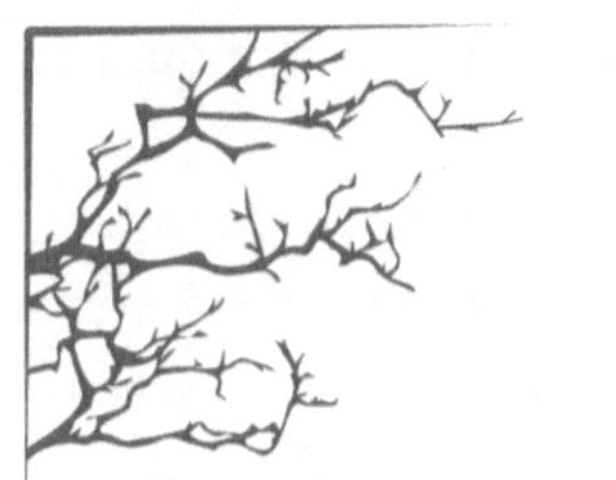

5

Lydia forced herself from bed. Sheryl and Warren would arrive in less than an hour. She thanked God for no phone calls the night before, allowing the much-needed sleep required for the day ahead. After she showered, her friends arrived. They came with food, determined to make her eat before they left for the cemetery. Comfort warmed her as she thought of her two mother hens.

She had taken her last bite of a muffin when Riley knocked. His expression was drawn and tired. Lydia sometimes forgot how her husband's death affected him. They had been close, and the last few weeks of Justin's life, Riley spent almost as much time at his bedside as Lydia.

"Thank you for coming."

She pecked his cheek before gathering a bouquet of white lilies from the table. They sparkled in the sunlight, bouncing in from the sliding glass doors. Riley took her elbow as the four somberly crawled into his dark blue Oldsmobile Cutlass. There were only a few times a year Riley changed from his uniform. Today, he wore a black jacket over a white shirt tucked into a pair of blue jeans. His black hat lay on the dashboard of the car.

Riley embraced her clenched fist when he drove through the double wrought-iron gates.

Lydia stared out at the faded stones. During the Civil War, everything in Lincolnville had been destroyed except the cemetery. The old mausoleums still stood with their original marble, announcing the families lying within. Most visitors thought the town was named for

39

President Lincoln, but in actuality, it was named for the first minister who had arrived in the early 1800's.

Lydia's mind eventually wandered to Justin. The pain she'd endured during his long illness taught her she couldn't prevent certain events from occurring. Generally, she had a comfortable life. While she still grieved for Justin, she'd gotten past his death. At least she had until the awful phone calls and an unannounced attraction for another man brought guilt. She prayed that after today, things would return to normal.

The car pulled to a stop in front of the large cement mausoleum. Pendleton was engraved across the top of the large stone pillar. It held the remains of Lydia's grandparents. Justin's headstone stood thirty feet away, under a large oak tree. A mixed arrangement of flowers sat at the base of his stone. Under the vase was a manila envelope.

"What do you suppose is in this?" Sheryl lifted it from the ground. "Maybe someone left a picture of themselves with Justin?"

Lydia's heart warmed at the kind gesture. However, anxiety rose when Riley handled the envelope at its edges.

Using a pen, he slid the flap open and pulled out a photograph of Matthew and Lydia walking from the church to her car. The word "mine" sprawled across Lydia's figure.

The air left her lungs, and she became lightheaded. Her hands trembled and the large stones hazed in her view. Her gaze darted, determined to locate her menace. He had to be watching, otherwise where would the fun be? Anger rushed in at this maniac for picking this particular day to be vicious. She felt Sheryl's arm support her.

"Maybe we should take her home," Warren said.

"No. She can do this," Sheryl spoke into Lydia's ear. "For Justin."

Lydia leaned her head against Sheryl's, refocusing on the day, and why she was there. "Thank you," she said, determined to hold herself together.

A deep breath of oxygen filled her lungs as she knelt at her husband's gravesite. Yes, she could do this, and would do it for Justin. There's no way she'd let some maniac chase her away.

She placed the flowers she'd been holding beside the grave marker. Kissing her palm, she held it against his name on the cold white stone. Finally, she stood, her chin up and head proud, not giving this phantom the satisfaction of thinking he'd won.

MATTHEW'S JAW CLENCHED shut. Who would play such a cruel prank?

"Looks like it was taken with the camera on a cell." Riley pulled the photograph from a file he brought in, laying it on the desk. "I guess I'm hoping you saw something, a car maybe, and might not have considered it important then."

Matthew glanced from the picture to Riley. Dark circles lay beneath his eyes. He sat in the same brown swivel chair as a few days before. His loose tie draped off to the side, and his clothes hung rumpled over his body.

"After your call, I went over the scenario in my mind." Matthew seethed at seeing the word scrawled upon Lydia's picture. "There wasn't anyone hanging around, whether in a car or not, that I remember. Any prints?"

"Mine and Sheryl's. The envelope came from an office supply store in Chattanooga." Riley pulled more information from the file. "No surprise they supply to mostly local businesses in Chattanooga."

"What is the surprise?" Matthew replaced the picture in the envelope before sitting in the high-back chair behind the desk. "There has to be more, or you wouldn't have driven across town. Small as it is, Lincolnville does have telephones."

"They also supply the Sheriff's Office here in Lincolnville." Riley stood and walked to the window. His shoulders folded as he leaned against the sill. "It would have been easy to get in, grab one or two without being noticed. We keep the place open when we're out on a call."

"Why go to that trouble when you can as easily buy one at Wal-Mart?"

"It only makes sense that it's someone from my office." Riley brushed a hand down his face. "A person I work with and see every day."

"You got anyone in mind?"

"No. It's not like there's a lot to choose from. We're just a small satellite office. The few who work for me are people I trust. Even those staffed at the main station in Ringgold are all good people."

"That's tough." Matthew rose. "I have a feeling that's not what's really bothering you."

Riley sighed and turned. His eyes held distress. "How do I tell Lydia that the people she should be able to trust the most might actually be the people she should trust the least?"

THE NEXT DAY, MATTHEW stood at Lydia's door, wishing he had called her instead. He had to fight this feeling of trepidation. Just thinking about Charlie's picture on Lydia's mantle upset his stomach. However, as her minister, he had to console her and make sure she was doing well.

"Well good morning, Pastor." Sheryl smiled with a quirk at the side of her mouth as she greeted him. "Fancy stumbling across you at the door this early."

"I heard what happened yesterday and thought I'd stop by to check on Ms. Frederickson."

"Ms. Frederickson. So formal. I'd be inclined to believe you'd at least be on a first name basis after you walked her to her car the other day." Sheryl ushered him in. "From the implications of that snapshot, she's the whore of Babylon." Her curt tone told him of her concern and anger.

As hard as Matthew tried to ignore it, he glanced at the picture of Charlie Westerman. He swore the young man's eyes glared back at him.

"Let the man at least have some coffee before you attack him." Lydia rounded the corner.

His heart stopped when he saw her. Even with all the anxiety she must be feeling, she still captured his breath. She led him and Sheryl into the kitchen. White painted walls held stainless steel appliances, giving the kitchen a contemporary look. Wood flooring traveled over the entire kitchen and dining room area. Two high stools with white cushioned seats sat scooted from underneath the white granite island.

"Riley told me about the photograph," Matthew said, grateful they moved to a room without no photographs. "I wanted to check on you."

"I've calmed a bit since I first saw the thing." She offered him a cup of coffee, which he accepted. "I'm trying to work myself up to being just angry today."

"Because of the picture, Riley's taking the calls more seriously than just a prank." Matthew pulled a seat out from under the island. He lifted the cup of coffee to his lips. The steam formed a wet mask across his nose.

"I'm not sure about that. It bothered me, though." Her voice lowered. "Sheryl spent the night. I guess she figured if the caller tried anything, she could protect me."

"Who needs a nice-looking sheriff when you have me?" Sheryl looped her arm through Lydia's as they stood against the countertop. It contrasted nicely with the rich brown cupboards.

Lydia started when a knock at the door sounded. Irritation grew inside Matthew. No one should be afraid in their own home.

Matthew rose. "You ladies sit; I'll get that." He forced himself not to look at Charlie as he went to answer the door.

Warren held a bag marked Betty's Bakery as he stood on the stoop. Matthew inhaled the aroma of warm blueberries.

"Pastor, what are you doing here?" Warren made his way into the foyer. "Nothing's happened to Lydia, has it?"

"No, she's inside having coffee. Sheryl's with her. I believe she'll be happy for you to join us."

"Hello, ladies." Warren gave Lydia a kiss on the cheek, then did the same for Sheryl. "I didn't realize the pastor would be here. I only bought three muffins." He took the stool Matthew had previously occupied.

"That's okay. I ate breakfast not too long ago," Matthew replied. "One of the perks of living at Anna's. I only stopped by to check on Lydia."

"Well, I'm fine, and I've decided not to let this guy bother me anymore," she said. "I've been feeling out of control, and I'm not going to let that happen anymore, either. The anniversary passed, and I've decided to move forward." Lydia gave a slight nod of determination.

"I agree," Warren said. "That's why I've taken your advice and accept that position I've been offered in Seattle."

"I'm glad." Lydia patted him on the shoulder. "We can't let this creep ruin either of our lives."

"What position is that?" Matthew leaned against the inner doorjamb of the kitchen.

"I'll be working for A Higher Calling in Seattle. It's a large computer graphics company that specializes in Christian work."

"He'll even be in charge of his own department." Pride carried in Sheryl's voice.

"I'm somewhat familiar with it. According to a weekly news magazine, it's one of the top places to work in this country." If Matthew remembered correctly, computer geeks were supposed to be ninety-pound weaklings. Warren was anything but. His large frame spoke of a weightlifter with his large biceps, broad shoulders, and small waist. He would do well with the workout nuts in Seattle.

"I still hate to leave with everything that's happening," Warren said. "If you want, I'll stay."

Expectation shone over Warren's face. His expression said he hoped she would ask him to stay. No one else appeared to realize it but Matthew.

"No, you will not." Lydia placed her hands on her hips. "You will go, enjoy your new job, and meet that special someone to spend the rest of your life with."

"Seattle's a nice city," Matthew said. "I have a friend out there who runs a local church. I'll get you his number so you can contact him. He'll make you feel welcome."

"That's settled." Lydia said with a smile. "You have a new job and possibly already a new place to worship. When do you need to leave?"

"In four weeks. They want the position filled as soon as possible." While Warren tried to stay light, Matthew caught the pain behind his smile.

As much as he hated to, Matthew knew he had to leave. Again, he felt that pang of wanting to spend more time with Lydia. But he tucked away those feelings. "Speaking of jobs, if I don't get back to work, I'll be joining Warren in Seattle. I hope to see you all Sunday. And best of luck to you, Warren." Matthew extended his hand. Warren returned a limp handshake, catching Matthew off guard considering Warren's stature.

"Let me walk you out." Lydia followed Mathew to the front door. "Thank you for coming by."

"I wanted to make sure you were all right." He placed his finger on the side of her chin. She looked exquisite. At first, Lydia appeared receptive to his touch, but a steely look jumped into her eyes.

Why did he get his signals so mixed up when it came to her? He could usually read other people well, particularly the opposite sex.

Before his Christian days, he'd had lots of practice. But his appraisal of Lydia proved difficult. She acted receptive to his touch, but then flinched as if burned by it.

"I'm happy for Warren." Lydia glanced over her shoulder. "We've been friends since grade school. It's going to be hard once he goes."

"I'm sorry, but it sounds like an excellent opportunity for him."

"Yes, it is. I'll miss him, that's all."

Matthew rode to work with a feeling of distress for Warren. Only one word described his expression: misery. Warren had probably imagined Lydia would fling her arms over his neck, proclaiming how much she loved him and beg him to stay. It was hard to find out the woman you adored didn't feel the same. Matthew's gut lurched as he recalled how she recoiled from his touch.

"God," he prayed. "Please help me fight these feelings I seem to have for this woman, because it's only a matter of time until I discover what Warren's going through."

LYDIA STOOD IN THE living-room, trying to get her senses back once Matthew left. His touch had been warm against her face. It felt pleasant having the touch of masculine skin against her own. But when Lydia caught sight of Justin's photograph, she jerked away. Matthew had to notice it. She gulped in a deep breath and returned to her two friends' stares.

"Well," Sheryl said.

"Well, what?" Lydia struggled to hide the tremor moving through her body.

"He stopped by after hearing about the picture." Sheryl tilted her head a bit to the side. Lydia remained silent, so she continued. "He made a point of coming by to check on you."

"It's no big deal. He did what most pastors would do. He visited a member of his congregation who's having a problem," Lydia explained. "Riley told him what happened at Justin's grave."

"It seems she's the only parishioner he's visited since he took over the church." Sheryl beamed.

"Not once either. Twice." Warren piped in.

"And I'm not aware of him walking one other person out to their car." Sheryl added with a large grin.

"Knock it off you two. It doesn't mean a thing." Lydia struggled to hide the smile working its way over her lips.

"Oh, my." Sheryl rose. "You like him too."

"If you continue, you'll make her crimson." Warren gave a quick eye roll.

"Lydia, it's great you like him. After all, he's a nice man, awesome looking, obviously very caring. And boy, what a bod!"

"Sheryl!" Lydia might have been thinking the same thing, but she wasn't about to say it out loud.

"What? He does."

"Is it blasphemy to say a preacher has a nice body?" Warren cracked in.

They paused, looking at each other before laughter erupted. Sheryl returned to the stool next to Warren.

"So, admit it," Sheryl said. "You're attracted to him. And he to you."

"But whenever I'm near him, I feel like I'm cheating on Justin." Lydia turned and glanced out the kitchen window. The pink flowers in the endless summer hydrangea were blooming. A lump rose in her throat. Justin had planted them shortly after they moved in.

"It's not cheating. Justin's been gone a long time. You've got to move on." Sheryl joined Lydia as they stared out the window. "And I have a feeling he and Matthew would have gotten on well."

"But talking about Matthew, in this house, in *our* house, it doesn't seem fitting." Lydia ran her palm along the kitchen counter. "He refinished this kitchen himself, with his sweat and hard work."

"Now you stop that." Sheryl pulled Lydia around and took her hands in her own. "This is your house, too." Sheryl wiped at a tear on Lydia's cheek. "This has nothing to do with you, with Justin, or with Matthew. This has to do with some weirdo out there trying to make you feel bad."

"It's working," Lydia whispered.

"IT'S HIM, AGAIN," PHYLLIS said.

Matthew had barely taken a step inside the church. He knew the "him" Phyllis spoke of was James Newman, III, who'd called several times regarding his son, Jimmy. Someone had set a couple of appointments for Matthew to meet with him, and so far, Jimmy had avoided every meeting.

"Let me guess, you forgot to turn your cell on again?" Phyllis let out a sigh. "I wish I could forget to turn on these phones sometimes."

"Could be a mistake." Matthew grinned. "Or at the very least, a Freudian slip."

Matthew liked Phyllis Baker. As he stood before her, he recalled how, on his first day, she told him exactly what he could expect from her.

"During football season, I will not be available for any Fridays or Saturdays that the Georgia Bulldogs play a home game," she said. "My husband and I tailgate, and since neither one of us really needs to work, we don't allow it to interfere."

Her voice brought him back to the present.

"It's funny you seem to forget that phone when James is trying to reach you," Phyllis added as Matthew strolled into his office. "Or it is because you were visiting Lydia Frederickson?"

"Hello, James. How are you today?" Matthew felt warmth rise into his cheeks. He had turned off his cell before entering Lydia's. He tried to convince himself it was so he wouldn't be rude by having a telephone ring while he checked on her. His real reason was his desire to keep distractions to a minimum, and he just *chose* to ignore James' calls, whether with Lydia or elsewhere.

"I've called several times." James' irritation became evident as he spoke. "Everyone is aware of you being at Lydia Frederickson's house after it was barely light out. As a reminder, you're on a ninety-day trial period. Spending more time working and not chasing our local widows would be a smarter move."

"I'm not chasing Ms. Frederickson. And so far, you're the only person complaining." Matthew looked up at the ceiling. *Why is patience a virtue God, when slamming down a telephone should be?* "I assume your call isn't to lecture me about my visitation. What can I do for you?"

"It's Jimmy. He feels up to stopping by today."

"Tell him I have a two o'clock available." Matthew believed Jimmy only told his father he'd come to counseling to appease him. By two, his tune would change.

"He should probably have an appointment for Monday, too."

"I'm afraid I'm out of the office on Mondays." Matthew flipped a page on his calendar. "I'm clear all-day Tuesday though."

"I forgot you take Mondays off." Hesitation lingered on the line. "As a new minister, I'm not sure dictating your days off is a good idea."

"I got approval from the committee when I was asked to lead the church. No one else seems bothered by it." From the start, Matthew had been fully aware he wasn't James' pick as the new minister. When the other committee members voted him in, James had no choice but to tolerate their decision. His tolerance appeared to be ending.

"I'll inform Jimmy about today. You can discuss Tuesday when he's there." James hung up without another word.

Dealing with Jimmy reminded Matthew of his days with the DEA. He knew Jimmy would never recover from his drug addiction unless he worked at quitting. He needed counseling, or it was only a matter of time until he fell into his old habits, if he hadn't already.

The vision of Charlie Westerman flashed into Matthew's mind. His heart pounded against his ribcage at the memory of Charlie lying dead beside his motorcycle.

Was James aware Matthew was responsible for Charlie's death? James had made it clear he didn't want Matthew as the pastor. If he knew, wouldn't he make certain of telling Lydia?

Matthew ran a hand down his face. He knew he had no choice. He had to tell her himself.

He rose and walked into the sanctuary. Taking a seat in the first pew, he stared up at the cross.

"God, the Bible says you never give us more than we can handle. I really need you to help me with the right words to tell Lydia how her brother died without causing her further pain." Matthew leaned forward, resting his elbows on his legs, and listened. He heard nothing but silence.

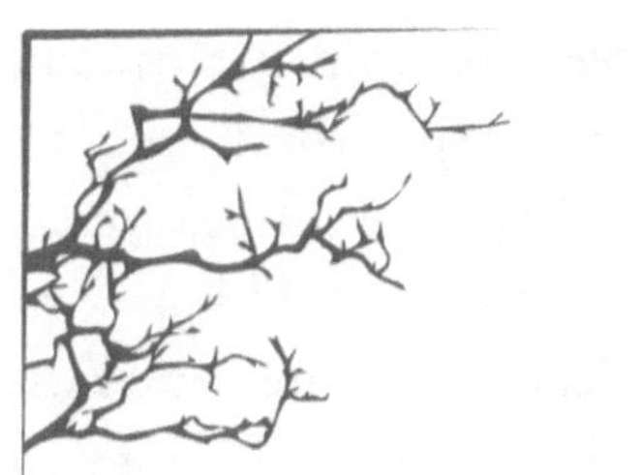

6

"Here we are." Matthew pulled into the space marked Guest Parking. A slight breeze blew his hair when he opened the door to the car.

It had been a little over three weeks since Matthew arrived in Lincolnville. He and his father had spent one day a week visiting assisted living facilities. His dad didn't require twenty-four-hour supervision, but Matthew wanted him in a place where someone could check on him daily.

Currently, his father lived with Brenda, but she already carried a full load with two kids. Matthew's apartment at Anna's Boarding House wasn't very large, or he would bring him to Lincolnville. A nearby pastor recommended Shady Gardens in Chattanooga.

The three-story facility was quite large, surrounded by perfectly aligned hedges. A brick walkway stretched to the large, white double-hung doors. Elderly people sat in rocking chairs on the front porch, watching others play croquet in the side yard. The outside was impressive with its large oak trees, but Matthew knew looks could be deceiving. The quality of care mattered most.

"It doesn't look too bad." His dad climbed from the car. "Pretty nicely shaded. It could do."

"Let's take a look inside." Matthew's father didn't want to burden his family, but Matthew wasn't going to rush into a living arrangement, and have his dad not receive the quality of care the man deserved.

They met with the administrator, Claudia Hugestein, at the front desk. She extended her thin fingers to Matthew's father. Matthew presumed the tall woman to be in her mid-fifties. Her green eyes gave

51

her no stand out features, unlike Lydia's violet eyes, which carried in his thoughts day and night. He had only seen her sporadically the last couple of weeks. With each occurrence, his heart would beat out a rhythm he was unfamiliar with. Yet she appeared to avoid him with every close encounter, indicating to him she had little desire to be with him. That was probably a good thing with the secret of her brother's death hanging between them.

"This is our game room," Ms. Hugestein said. Two men glanced up from the cards in their hands and nodded. "Our cook has yet to have a complaint, and she can fix your meal with any special medical requests needed." The cafeteria carried a slight odor of meatloaf.

"I don't require anything special," Dad said.

Matthew glanced around. Comfort rose when they entered the library and several Bibles stood upright on the bookcase.

As they rounded the corner toward the large screened-in porch, an aroma he'd become all too familiar with grabbed him. The smell of gardenias enveloped him, causing the thumping in his chest to sound all the way to his ears. It's bad enough he had Lydia on his mind constantly, but she was all over his senses.

"This is one of our volunteers," Ms. Hugestein said. "She comes by once a week to visit with our residents."

Matthew's heart leapt into his throat as he looked into soft blue-violet eyes.

LYDIA ADJUSTED THE footrests on Ms. Mouldune's wheelchair when it hit her. Spice, an aroma she dreamt of. She lost her balance and nearly toppled over.

"Darling, is everything all right? You look a bit flushed," Ms. Mouldune said.

"Something crossed my mind." Lydia did her best to calm her voice. "I hope he was handsome."

Ms. Mouldune patted Lydia on her forearm. She felt her cheeks heat.

"This is one of our volunteers." Ms. Hugestein stood behind her. "She comes by once a week to visit with our residents."

As Ms. Hugestein introduced her, Lydia bid Ms. Mouldune goodbye. Lydia's throat constricted as she saw two sets of piercing sapphire blue eyes. The older gentleman clearly had to be Matthew's father.

Osteoporosis had taken its toll on the older man, causing a slouch in his upper body. His shoulders drooped forward, and the hump-like curve of his back told of his age.

"Lydia, this is Pastor Matthew Winters and his father, George. Mr. Winters is considering joining out little group here."

"I've already met Matthew. He's our new minister. However, it's nice to meet you, Mr. Winters."

Lydia shook hands with Matthew's father. He accepted with frail, silk fingers. He had the same firm jaw as his son, and she imagined years earlier, the same dark hair color. Still attractive, the grayness of the hair and his wrinkles gave him a more distinguished look with his advanced age.

"Son, you better call the funeral parlor." Mr. Winters chuckled. "I must have died because I've met an angel of God's."

"Don't let the persona fool you." Lydia leaned closer to the older man. "There are horns holding up this halo."

Mr. Winters let out a loud laugh.

"You volunteer here every week?" Mr. Winters smiled.

"I try my best," Lydia said.

"Where do I sign up?" He gave her a wink. "I don't think I've ever seen such a pretty young lady. I imagine you receive plenty of trouble from the men here."

"They usually behave themselves once I demonstrate my bite." Lydia chomped her teeth together. "I hope your son didn't drive you over on that motorcycle of his."

Mr. Winters smiled. "No, I wouldn't be able to hold on very well. We drove my car."

Lydia swallowed hard and finally turned to Matthew. "And how are you today?"

"I'm doing fine. You?"

"Good." Lydia bit her tongue to hide the elation she felt when Matthew took her hand in a firm handshake.

"Lydia, why don't you show Mr. Winters our garden?" Ms. Hugestein said. "This way I can speak with his son."

"It will be my pleasure." Lydia was glad for a moment's reprieve from Matthew. She directed Mr. Winters to the patio area. "I hope you enjoy roses, because this place is full of them."

"If they're as pretty as you, I'll adore them."

Lydia strolled through the garden, showing Mr. Winters where seasonal flowers and vegetables were grown. After walking around the cement path in the middle of the grounds, she guided him to a nearby bench where they could sit and take in the view.

"Boy, your husband is a very lucky man." He held up her left hand with the wedding band.

"I'm a widow." Lydia explained.

"Oh, I'm sorry. You're too young to have gone through that." Mr. Winters paused. "It's a hard loss to recover from, losing someone you love that much."

"Yes, it is." Lydia bit back tears. "It's not a feeling a person who's divorced could ever understand."

"No. No, it isn't."

He shook his head. The old man's gaze held a faraway look. It was the same one Lydia had when she recalled her time with Justin.

"Will there be a time when it won't hurt so much?" She hoped the subject wasn't too painful.

"Yes. After a while, all you remember are the pleasant things."

Lydia couldn't wait until that day finally arrived.

"So, what do you think of our gardens, Mr. Winters?" Ms. Hugestein walked up with Matthew and joined them.

"Almost as pretty as this young lady seated beside me."

"I'm glad to hear that," Ms. Hugestein said. "Lydia, would you care to show Pastor Winters the park while I speak to his father?"

As much as Lydia wanted to shout no, she agreed. She then led Matthew through the wrought-iron gate, then across the street to Shady Gardens Park. She glanced over at a group of children playing on the jungle gym. Their laughter echoed in the warm air.

"Good size park," Matthew said, breaking the silence.

"It's two and a half acres. A family in Atlanta donated all the property to the retirement center. They had a parent at Shady Gardens and offered the park as a way to say thank you for the excellent care." Lydia had a feeling she was rambling, but hoped it kept her emotions at bay. "Your dad's very sweet." Lydia then added. "You have his eyes."

"Really? I hadn't noticed."

She stopped and looked up at him. "You're not aware of the distinct eye color you and your father share?"

"Not that I recall."

"I'm surprised none of your girlfriends mentioned it. It's something a woman would take notice of, more so than a man."

"He's never met any of my girlfriends. You're the first woman in my life he's ever met."

Tenderness rushed over her as they proceeded forward. His words uplifted her. She tried to convince herself meeting his dad was pure coincidence. After all, if she let it mean more, she would have to admit she had feelings for Matthew. Emotions she wasn't prepared to allow in yet.

A SMILE INCHED OVER Lydia as they walked. Matthew wanted to be the reason for it. It had been several days since he'd seen her, but she still haunted his dreams. He prayed when they saw each other next, he'd find the right words to talk about Charlie's death. However, now, alone with her, words escaped him.

"The weather is wonderful." She inhaled loudly. "It feels great being outside."

"I haven't seen you out much in Lincolnville. There's a nice park I run in everyday."

"I have my reasons for not being seen outside there."

Matthew stopped mid-step. "I'm sorry. It has to be hard believing you have someone watching you."

"It's pretty evident from the phone calls. They started again a few days after receipt of the picture. I even got a new unlisted number, but it did no good. He mentions how I wore my hair while out or talks about items I bought at the store."

A stone sat in the pit of Matthew's stomach. She had to be frightened whenever she left her house. The last thing she needed to hear now was how her minister killed her brother. But once they found who was stalking her, he'd find a way to tell her.

"Riley's doing the best he can to figure out who it is," she said. "But the person is pretty technologically savvy. Apparently, he's calling through a computer link, and that's why they can't identify him. He's now phoning both my landline and my cell. And the caller ID shows a different business each time. When I dial back, a recording says it's not accepting incoming calls."

Her vulnerable demeanor appeared to be mixed with dread.

"Well, it looks like it's just you and me here, so you can enjoy yourself."

He offered her his arm. She accepted, slipping her arm through his. A shower of warmth nestled over him when she smiled up at him. A warning inside summoned, advising him to distance himself, or he would pay the price in the end. However, he chose not to listen.

A slight breeze blew Lydia's hair into her face. When she shook her head, the strands draped across her shoulders, looking soft and delightful to touch. He longed to feel its silkiness.

They finally stopped on a small bridge overlooking a brook. The water flowed beneath, everything peaceful. Matthew pulled Lydia's hair from her face, gently caressing her cheek with his knuckles. She leaned toward his touch. As she stared at him, her expression became dreamy and inviting. He moved toward her, feeling her warm breath stroke his cheek. Not a word was spoken as they neared. Their lips traveled within seconds of meeting. A union Matthew yearned to create. Then all at once, she shrank away.

"I can't. Please." She backpedaled; her tone turned sharp. "I can't do this, not now." Her jaw locked as she trotted off toward Shady Gardens.

Matthew stood leaning against the bridge's rail, seething with frustration. What could he be thinking? Therein lay the problem. No thinking was involved. If he had been, he wouldn't have allowed his emotions to go that far. Here he stood, a minister, not some young stud out trying to pick up a babe in the park. He had to reign in his desire, and fast, before he jeopardized his walk with God.

Besides, he couldn't get involved with her without first telling her about shooting Charlie. Lydia would never want to be with a man responsible for the death of her brother.

Exhaling loudly, he trudged to the retirement home. The way she had his insides bouncing about, he'd have thought he was on a trampoline. First, she was warm and sweet, then she became an iceberg. He could have sworn she would allow the kiss until she flinched. How could she keep him tied in knots? The last thing he needed was some woman with a come-hither look, drawing him in, only to push him away.

Maybe he shouldn't bother with his love life right now. If his past record was any indication, a relationship with Lydia would turn out bad. She was beautiful, and before he found God, he certainly would have made a play for her with the hopes of getting her into bed. However, he hadn't been physically involved with a woman since he came to Jesus. Matthew peeked at his watch to figure the exact moment.

"But who's counting?" he said out loud to himself. God and his congregation were where his focus should be. He only hoped it would be that easy.

His father waited in a rocking chair on the front porch. They sat in silence as they drove to Brenda's house. Matthew decided he would drop his father off, hop on his bike, and return to his apartment. Staying for dinner would include his sister's questions about his personal life, something he wasn't in the mood to discuss.

"You've hardly said a word since you returned from the park." Dad looked over at his son. "Is everything all right?"

"Yes." Matthew felt remorse immediately for his curt tone and for the lie.

"You have feelings for her. Don't you?" His father's voice held concern. "It's understandable, son. She's not only attractive, but a nice lady to boot. You could do far worse than that one."

"It's that obvious?" Matthew exhaled and leaned against the headrest. "She's the only woman who makes me eager to see her one minute, and sorry I met her the next."

"I believe she has feelings for you, and it scares her." Dad continued. "You're probably the first man to really grab her attention since her husband passed away. She's got to be wondering how she can be attracted to you when the love of her life has died."

"You figured all that out from the brief talk you had?"

"I gathered that from the way she looked at you with a mixture of excitement and pain. Every person who's lost a spouse knows of those guilt feelings. You're afraid if you go on you're not doing justice to their memory." He patted his son's forearm. "Talk to her. Explain your feelings and give her some time. Most importantly, pray. God and time are the two best healers there are."

Matthew was shocked and impressed by his father's knowledge. He smiled as he recalled a quote from Mark Twain: "When I was a boy of fourteen, my father was so ignorant I could hardly stand to have the old man around. But when I got to be twenty-one, I was astonished at how much the old man had learned in seven years."

"I'll think about it," Matthew said. "Maybe I should just focus on the church."

"Is there a problem? You've never been one to shirk away from anything, especially a woman." Dad laughed. "Sometimes talking about it can help."

Matthew didn't want to talk about it. He hadn't told his family about shooting an innocent man when it happened, and he sure wasn't in the mood to tell him now.

"I'm just thinking about what you said."

Matthew measured his father's words. Something had definitely drawn him to Lydia, and he knew deep down she felt the same.

She obviously didn't know the name of the officer who shot Charlie, or she would have said something when they first met. Unless someone did some deep research, it might never come out. Could he actually get to know her and keep this a secret?

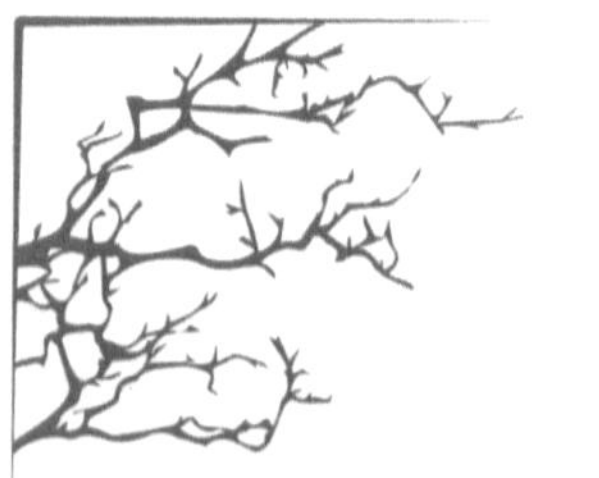

7

A little before four, Lydia pulled her blue Honda Civic onto the highway. She couldn't drag her mind from the near kiss she and Matthew came close to sharing. She couldn't let that happen again. Her life had too much going on with prank phone calls and her job to become involved in a relationship. Especially with someone who had her all mixed up emotionally.

How was he able to reach out and touch her in places that hadn't been touched in a long time? They were walking and talking, carrying on a pleasant conversation, then in what seemed like seconds, they were close to being in each other's arms. The tone of his voice was smooth and deep. It incited feelings in her she thought died with Justin. She knew she had to leave the park before it was too late. She had to keep that strength next time she bumped into Matthew. It had to be loneliness causing her to be so susceptible to him whenever he was near.

After passing Ringgold, white smoke clouded her view as steam escaped from her engine.

She grasped the steering wheel to regain control. The vehicle veered to the left-hand lane. She had been driving sixty, but now slowed considerably. A plume of smoke blocked her view. Her grip tightened.

"Please God," she pleaded. "Don't let me veer into oncoming traffic."

Cars honked as she pulled to the side of the road. Her nerves jittered as she gained her composure. Popping the hood release before climbing from the car, she frowned as she examined the engine. She knew absolutely nothing about cars, so the action had been pointless. She pulled out her cell and dialed the auto club. The lady on the phone

60

told her it would be a thirty-minute wait, so she returned to the car and pulled out a book to read.

A loud roar from behind the car startled her. Against her will, her heart stepped up its tempo. "Stop that," she scolded as Matthew tugged his helmet off. The way her emotions acted; you would think he was a white knight. She said in a low tone, "Don't forget he's not on a white horse, and bad guys wear black in the movies."

"What's wrong?" Matthew held the door as she pulled herself from the car.

"I have no idea. It just started smoking from the engine. I have a tow truck coming. They should be here in about..." She twisted her wrist, glancing at her watch. "About ten minutes ago."

"Let's have a look." Matthew removed his jacket, revealing a tight, long-sleeved polo shirt. The fabric stretched over his biceps as he leaned over the engine. He then sprawled on the ground, looking under the car.

"I'm not the best mechanic, but I'd say it's your radiator."

Lydia scooted back to the passenger side door as far from Matthew as could be reasonable without being obvious.

"Do you have a mechanic?" Matthew hollered from the ground.

"I usually take it to the dealership in Chattanooga."

"They'll probably be closed now. I have a brother-in-law in Ringgold who owns a shop. I'll give him a call and check whether he can be of service."

"I appreciate that."

Glad somewhat for Matthew's company, she sat on a large rock between the vehicle and the motorcycle. She'd had too many butterflies earlier to eat lunch, and her stomach reminded her as it grumbled for food. White clouds floated in the blue sky. She wondered how fun they were to jump upon.

"My brother-in-law said he'll take care of it for you." Matthew sat on the ground beside her.

"You can go on. I'll have the tow truck driver take me over to his garage." His cologne blew into her. Lydia had hoped he'd stay, but feared him being so near.

"I'm not about to leave you out here by yourself." Matthew reclined with his legs stretched out in front. "Besides, it'll allow us a moment to talk."

"About what?" Lydia's stomach twisting.

Matthew focused on the highway. "Us."

Lydia swallowed hard. The last thing she wanted was to have this conversation. She rolled the wedding band around her finger. The diamond from her engagement ring sparkled in the sun. She had to take control of her emotions. However, when she caught sight of Matthew returning a glance, her heart boomed in her chest. So much for being in control.

MATTHEW HADN'T REALIZED the topic would upset her until she went pale. Dread came over at the awareness he caused that type of reaction. Something inside cautioned him to go no further. He couldn't listen.

Or wouldn't.

The sun descended behind pine trees across the highway as Matthew prayed the proper words would form to explain how he felt. Only then did he realize how unclear his own feelings were. Quick and straightforward. That'd be the best method. He breathed deep before proceeding.

"I'll make it as painless as I can." He continued to watch cars on the highway, not wanting anything in her demeanor to distract him. "I have feelings for you. Though I'm not sure what they are, I know they're there. Whenever I see you, even just a glimpse, a nervous feeling comes over me. It's as if my heart's about to burst from my chest because it's pounding so hard. I'm having a tough time getting you off my mind."

He squinted in her direction, trying to glean a reading on her, wondering what effect his words were having. He couldn't tell. She just kept twisting her rings.

"It makes no sense why I feel this way. We met only a short time ago." Matthew returned his gaze to the highway. "I can't recall having these feelings before, so I'm pretty secure in the fact it's not hormones. At least not only hormones." He glanced back at her.

Lydia's lip went into a small grin. "I've never met a minister who talked about hormones."

"We all have them. Kind of silly not to bring them up if they're affecting us, especially to God and the person causing them to bounce like a ball in a pinball machine." Matthew stood. "I have no intention of pressuring you. I'm talking about becoming better acquainted. We might realize we're meant to be no more than friends."

Lydia remained silent as she stared down at her rings.

He shrugged. "That's my say. I'm not sure what to do with it, but there it is." Pressure that had been evident for days released itself from his insides. With any luck, she'd say she wasn't interested, and it would end here.

"I'm having feelings for you too," Lydia said. "The biggest problem is I feel I'm betraying Justin."

His heart skipped a beat at her words. However, his elation was short-lived. If she ever found out he killed her brother, it would end any type of relationship he could ever hope for. After a few seconds of silence, he spoke.

"That's natural. We'll have to work through it. Take things slow." Why did he not tell her to call when she was ready? He was acting like a blind man about to walk off a cliff.

"I'm not sure I can." Lydia murmured as she stared at the ground.

"I won't pressure you about any of this." He watched the tow truck's arrival. "Let's take care of your car, and we can talk some more over a bite to eat."

She touched his arm said, "I'm sorry."

"That's okay. Since I'm still pretty new in the area, I'll let you get me up to speed on the ins and outs of Lincolnville."

As the tow truck driver finished pulling Lydia's car onto the truck, she asked about a ride to the repair shop.

"I'm sorry; our insurance won't allow any riders." He unhooked the winch from the car.

"I'll give you a ride," Matthew said.

"On that thing?" Lydia pointed to the two-tone motorcycle.

"It's perfectly safe. And I promise to drive careful. I'll also let you use my helmet."

"I guess there isn't much of a choice."

Matthew's palms sweated as he hooked the black helmet under her chin. He opened the left saddle bag attached to the bike for her purse.

"Is that a Bible?" She stared at the thick red book inside.

"Sure is. There's one on each side. It gives me a secure feeling." He opened the other bag to show the black book.

She laughed. "It reminds me of a Toby Keith song about riding on a motorcycle with a Bible."

Matthew sought to control the palpitations he felt as she climbed on behind him, her arms gripping around his torso. When they wrenched forward as he accelerated, she grabbed even tighter. With her arms clutched around, her breath bounced against his neck. Matthew decided, at that moment, he would stop at nothing to become more familiar with this woman. No matter how loud that alarm inside him sounded.

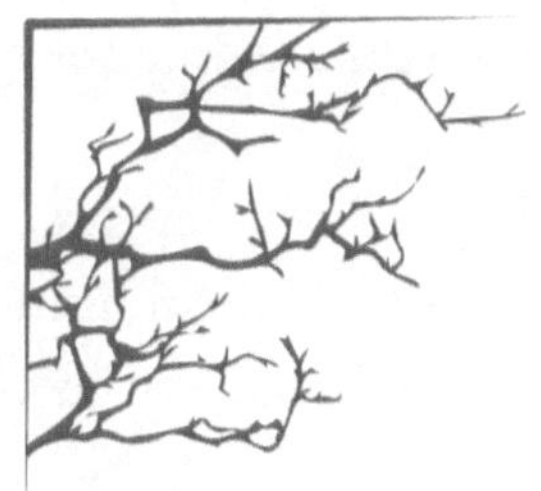

8

Lydia tightened her grip around Matthew as they flew down the highway. The wind raced over her body. Trees cast a green blur as they sped by. The ride both frightened and excited. It reminded her of when she rode the roller coaster at Six Flags as a kid. The experience thrilled her. She was unsure if it was from the motorcycle ride or being so near Matthew.

They pulled into Petry's Automotive off the main road in Ringgold, Georgia. Matthew held out his hand for her to take as she climbed off the bike. Her fingers warmed beneath his.

"How'd you like the ride?" He waited until she removed the helmet before continuing. "You enjoyed it. Come on, fess up."

"You're a wonderful preacher." Came her reply, with a sly grin.

"Why do you say that?"

"Because you scared the devil out of me." She laughed.

His hair stood in disarray from the wind, but it worked for him. "That's a wonderful sound," Matthew said. He moved a loose wave of hair that had drooped over Lydia's forehead.

"What sound is that?" Lydia became aware of her staring in a way that made her self-conscious.

"The sound of you laughing."

His words, earlier, by the side of the road expressed what she'd been feeling for days but was afraid to admit. She only hoped she could manage her emotions. When Matthew told her his heart beat out of his chest whenever he saw her, it caused goose bumps to run over her arms.

When they entered the building, Matthew introduced her to his brother-in-law Richard Petry, a big man standing at least six-foot-five, then suggested they eat at a sandwich shop on the corner while they waited to hear about her car.

The small deli held only four round tables. Beneath each sat three wrought-iron chairs with barely enough padding to prevent them from being uncomfortable. They placed their order, before taking a seat in a table farthest from the front.

"So, how long have you lived in Lincolnville?" Matthew slipped off his jacket.

"Most of my life. My grandparents moved there shortly after they married. My mom and dad are Lincolnvillians."

"Tell me about your family." Matthew leaned against the back of the chair.

"Why? Are you looking for donations?" Lydia teased.

"No. The more I know about my parishioners, the better it helps me to understand them. Things like what type of environment they were raised in, how close they are with their families?"

"I grew up in a fabulous environment. Two loving parents, no harsh times, really, until I became a teen. My brother got killed when I was seventeen. But other than that, I had a wonderful childhood. Hard to believe with how crazy my life has been." Lydia gave off a slight laugh that held no humor.

Matthew fidgeted with a straw wrapper. "Were you and your brother close?"

"Somewhat. He got into drugs, and it changed our relationship. He was killed in some sort of drug sting. I'm not sure what really happened. I have good memories of him when he was younger." She gulped back tears. "Enough of Charlie. My dad had worked for a computer company for years. He had significant benefits, including stock in the company. By his forty-eighth birthday, he'd saved enough to retire and buy the property on the hill. They built the ski lodge on the other side of the mountain."

"Wow, that's a big lodge." Matthew leaned back in the chair and let out a sigh. "Skiing. That's something I haven't done for a while."

"You'll have to go. It doesn't always have enough snow, so they make the fake stuff, but it's still fun." Lydia paused for a sip of her drink. "They leased it out a few years ago. They still own the land, but another couple took over the lodge and cabins. Part of the sale included them allowing the congregation to use a cabin for the youth two weeks every winter at no charge. It works out well."

"Now I want to know about you," he said.

"Not much to me." Lydia shrugged. "I create website logos from my office at the house. Not an abundance of excitement unless you mention my stalker."

"I say we ignore him for now," Matthew said. "What about your two friends, Sheryl and Warren?"

"Ah, you want the gossip." She raised her eyebrows up and down.

"Not gossip, the real stuff. Knowing about my congregation enables me to be the best minister I can be."

"Yeah, right." Lydia wiped condensation from her glass of sweat tea. "Sheryl's an only child. Our mothers are best friends from college. When my parents returned to Lincolnville, so did hers. They all live in Savannah now. Sheryl's grandparents left her a sizeable trust she lives on. She does volunteer work for hospice during the week. She also paints and sells out at the art fair held in the town every year. I have a cousin who also sells some of her paintings in Atlanta."

"Boy, she sounds busy, making fine use of her days."

"She's the person you should talk to for the inside scoop. She can apprise you of pretty much anything you want to know about anybody in the town. That comes from her being overly friendly. When she goes for a walk, which is almost every day, people stop her to talk. You wouldn't believe what they say about their neighbors. It's really pretty amazing."

"I'll bet. Tell me about Warren. I know he's getting ready to leave for a job in Seattle, but that's about all I know about him."

"He leaves in another week. We've known him since grade school. Unlike Sheryl, he's quieter and more reserved. He currently works for his stepdad over at Computer Sense. His dad abandoned the family when he was seven and his mother died a couple of years after remarrying. Donald Fisher raised him through his teen years. I believe there are a half-brother and sister out there somewhere, but he's only met them once. Of course, Sheryl and Warren argue and tease each other so much, you'd think they were siblings."

"It's great you three are so close." Matthew gulped his drink as he leaned an elbow on the table. "How well do you know Riley?"

Lydia smiled at the thought of Riley, who'd become a good friend. "Since Justin died, he's been a shoulder to lean on. We used to have him over for dinner, but he'd been more my husband's friend than mine. They had worked together on some cases in Atlanta. Justin was a state attorney.

"When the sheriff's office had an opening, he contacted Riley, thinking he might be interested. My mom had a lot of pull, and she took stock in Justin's opinion. They hired Riley the day he showed up. It ruffled a few feathers, but he's done a wonderful job, so the complaints have lessened." She chose not to mention that James Newman, III was the most vocal against Riley.

The lady behind the counter brought their order to the table. Lydia watched Matthew as he covered his cheeseburger in ketchup and mustard.

"You enjoy a little bit of hamburger with your ketchup, don't you?"

Matthew smiled. "What can I say? I'm a condiment type of guy."

Lydia adored the twinkle in his eyes when he smiled. It was both warm and impish. An explosion of sensations went off again. She had an urge to know him better, or at least she thought so. If only the confusion inside would dissipate to aid in her decision.

MATTHEW LEANED IN TO listen as Lydia talked about her relationship with her husband's friend. The more she talked, the more he realized how hard Justin's death must have been on Riley.

"Riley is somewhat of a loner. Women find him intriguing because he's quiet and a mystery to them," Lydia said. "He's not really that hard to figure out. He's serious and doesn't care for game players, which leaves out quite a few women."

"I'm wondering if a bunch of kids wouldn't loosen him up."

"Probably. He was close to a woman at one time, but she died in a robbery. Justin said it caused him to become severe. Apparently, he used to laugh and go out with friends before it happened, but all he does now is throw himself into his work. I can't remember if he's ever had a vacation."

Matthew shook his head. "That must have been terrible, being a cop and losing a person you care for to a crime you couldn't prevent."

"I can't think of a time I've ever heard him talk about his parents. The only family I know of is an aunt who visits from Jacksonville. He doesn't seem to have any family close to lean on. It took a tragedy like Justin dying for me to realize what a decent guy Riley is. Of course, I also had Sheryl and Warren beside me. They've kept me from hiding away these last couple of years." Lydia paused and took a drink. "Enough of me and mine. Let's talk about you? And I want something juicy because when I inform Sheryl about us having dinner, she'll want to hear all the details."

"You plan to fill Sheryl in about this?"

"Sheryl and I have no secrets."

Matthew hadn't realized she would divulge their earlier conversation. The idea made him anxious. And then a thought occurred to him. If Sheryl was as good as Lydia indicated at finding information, it would only be a matter of time until she found out about Matthew killing Lydia's brother. Someone in Lincolnville had to know. He didn't keep his DEA record a secret from the committee when he applied for the job, but no one mentioned anything about the incident in Miami. Matthew's stomach tied in a knot.

He swallowed down his unease and said, "Ask away. I'm an open book."

"How did you end up in Lincolnville? Most preachers we get are older, looking to retire."

"I'm fond of small towns. They have a charm to them. Big cities have too much bureaucracy instead of God. "

"I'm sure your sister living in Ringgold had something to do with your choice."

Matthew nodded. "When I visited a couple summers ago, I stopped off for a social call on Riley. The area is nice, so when an opening came up, he gave my name to a committee member as a candidate for the job."

"And what's your story on Riley?" She crunched a chip from her plate.

"We worked on a case in Atlanta involving drugs coming through the airport. It was an intricate operation between the pilots and people dealing with the cargo. They couldn't figure out who gave the orders. They brought me in undercover. Riley and I became fast friends. It works well when you have to trust the person handling the operation."

"You were a cop with the Atlanta Police Department, too?"

"Drug Enforcement Agency," he said. The words caught in his throat. Would she ask questions about her brother? "My work undercover is why I have the tattoos. It personified my angry I'll-do-anything-for-money-image" I had to establish." Matthew's voice lowered. "I'd probably have reconsidered if I'd known I'd end up in this line of work."

"That's quite a stretch, going from an undercover drug agent to a minister. It's always amazing the people God uses in His work." Lydia then added. "And the tattoos don't look that bad. Besides, it gives you an in with the kids. You're not like an ordinary preacher, so they might be more willing to listen to what you have to say."

"I hope so," Matthew said. "Kids need to understand how much their lives would improve if they accepted and lived for Christ."

Matthew breathed a sigh of relief as she skipped right over him being with the DEA. Since she was young when her brother died, she might not be aware a cop shot him.

"I agree." She leaned forward, and with a glint in her eye, said, "Now, to the really personal stuff. Are you as arrogant as you appear, or is that to cover for a lack of self-confidence?"

"Arrogant? What do you mean?" He felt as if a fist had gone into his gut. The worse part, no joke lay behind the question. Lydia was serious.

Lydia held up one finger. "First, you drive an extremely loud motorcycle, so everyone knows when you arrive. That either shows you need everyone to be aware you're there, or you do it so they can't miss you, and you won't be lost in the crowd."

"I bought it like that. I never considered changing it."

Matthew's discomfort level rose. He'd only felt worse than this one other time in his life. A picture of Charlie Westerman's body lying on the ground with a bullet in his forehead flashed into his mind. He shook his head to get the vision out.

"Maybe, but on the first day you came into the sanctuary, purposely dressed unconventional, no suit or tie. If your goal was to make everyone nervous, you succeeded. Then you proceed to preach about judging a book by its cover. You knew you'd surprise the congregation with the long hair, but you went overboard with the whole dark look."

"I do it to show that if a person wears unorthodox clothing or looks a certain way, it doesn't mean they aren't a Christian or someone worth saving." Matthew stared at her. The bite of his hamburger stuck in his throat.

"If you say so." Lydia leaned forward. "It couldn't be because you believed the congregation wouldn't accept you with long hair and a tattoo, could it? Instead of a suit, you went for shock. Somewhat judgmental on your part." She waved her index finger at him, a grin on her face.

Matthew forced his mouth to close. Lydia held a lilt in her words as if teasing, but he sat motionless, stunned by her words. Irritation grew inside.

They sat in silence for what seemed like minutes before he realized how correct her words were. Would the people in the diner still have cringed that first day, if instead of walking to the back, he had introduced himself to a few of them? Maybe he should review his own sermon. He might actually learn something from it.

This woman told him information about himself that wasn't clear to him before. It brought a chill along his spine. She had him figured out from the beginning, like she could see through to his inner thoughts, and he could barely read her. His breathing intensified as he stared at her.

"I hate to disturb you." Richard Petry yanked him from his thoughts. "But there's a pretty good size leak in your radiator. It needs to be replaced."

"How long will that take?" Lydia glanced over at Richard.

"The problem is I have to order it. I can't get it in until tomorrow."

"I'll give you a ride home," Matthew said.

"I guess I'll have Sheryl bring me back over tomorrow. I have to use the facilities, if you don't mind." Lydia nodded toward the ladies' room.

"Mind. You're sitting behind me on a motorcycle. I insist."

"You don't talk much like a preacher man." Lydia let out a laugh. She rose and headed toward the back of the cafe.

"And there it is, that smile again." Everything appeared to brighten when Lydia gave a half smile. "I'll swing by once I pick up the bike." He watched in silence as she walked away before turning to his brother-in-law. "So?"

"You called it." Richard hesitated. "The radiator was definitely tampered with."

Anger rose inside. Matthew hoped he'd been wrong. Once they returned to the garage, Richard led Matthew to the car still raised off the ground.

"They jabbed a hole in the bottom with, my guess from the size, would probably be a screwdriver." Richard pointed it out. "They then fidgeted with her temperature gage so it wouldn't show she was leaking water until it was too late. I'll take it out and give it to the cops to look at."

Matthew's fists tightened.

Richard shook his head. "I'd say whoever it was wanted to leave her stranded. Maybe out of spite. Or worse, he probably hoped she'd be alone so he could have her go with him, either by choice or force."

MATTHEW'S SCENT WAFTED over Lydia as he followed her up her steps. It was a smell she could get lost in.

He retreated to his bike after telling her goodnight. She had a hop in her step as she entered. It had been a while since she enjoyed getting out with someone new. The suggestion of slowly building a friendship grew on her.

She glanced at herself in a nearby mirror. Her hair lay flat on the top of her head. She ran her hands through, giving it some much needed volume. There's no way to keep a good style when you wear on a helmet.

When she passed through the living-room, a giggle escaped. She was as bad as a teenager who learned their crush also liked them. She tossed her shoes off and spun in a circle on the wood floor. Feeling attracted to another man had not been what she planned. It gave her a strange mixture of glee and guilt. They seemed to collide in her system. Sheryl's words resonated in her mind. Justin *would* want her to be happy and to go on with her life.

Matthew had an interesting history; one she would like to learn more about. When he spoke earlier of being undercover, she found herself relieved he no longer placed his life in danger.

At times, he'd seemed concerned about something else. His eyes glazed over for a moment, and he appeared to have a secret he wanted to tell her but didn't dare. She laughed out loud. She needed to quit reading those mystery novels, or she'd start to see a murder behind every door.

As she stepped into the kitchen, she noticed the blinking light on her answering machine indicating a message. Inside, she hoped it would be Matthew who left the message, but with him on a motorcycle, she doubted it. Most likely Sheryl. A neighbor probably called her about Matthew dropping her off. After taking a deep breath to prepare herself for one of Sheryl's interrogations, she pressed the button.

"How could you do that to your husband? Cheating on such a nice man. Walking in the park. Tsk, tsk. If you had kissed him, I would have had to teach you a lesson." Fear engulfed her at the sound of the stranger.

She dialed Riley, her fingers trembling.

"Hello."

"Riley. I got another phone call." Lydia tried to control the panic in her voice. "It's on my machine."

"I'm on my way," he said. "Until I get there, don't answer the door or the phone."

A cold sweat came over her. How long had he been watching her? Lydia's back pressed against the wall. Tears fell as she slid down the wall to the floor.

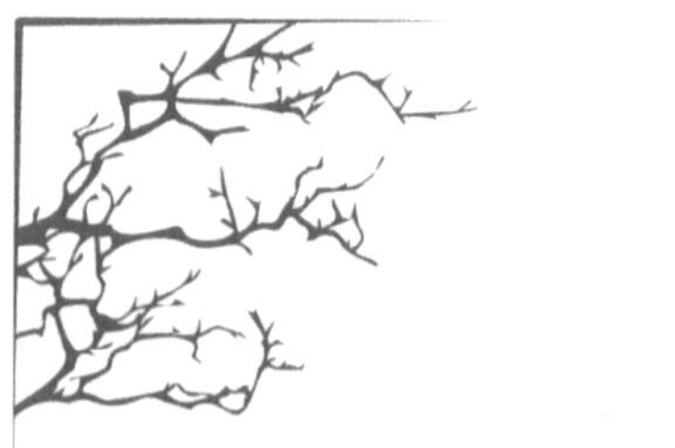

9

Matthew waited until he got home to call Riley about Lydia's radiator. The voicemail came on, so he left a message. There was only one explanation for the radiator—it had to be the person making the phone calls.

As Matthew recalled the conversation with Lydia in the sandwich shop, and how well she seemed to read him, his stomach did another flop. How could she be so correct about something that *he* hadn't even seen? He had been arrogant when he first arrived. He did all the things she had alleged. Her accusation of him acting as though he was a more devout Christian tore away at his nerves. That hadn't been his intention, but it had been the outcome.

How many other things had she'd picked up? Did she notice how on edge he became when talking about her brother? Matthew swallowed hard. He sat down in front of his laptop and ran an internet search on the name "Charlie Westerman". Several news articles scrolled up. He read through each one. There was no mention of his own name in any. They didn't even mention that the DEA was involved. They just referred to Charlie's death as an officer-involved shooting. Good. That left the field wide opened. It could have been anyone.

He strolled over to the small bay window in his room. The darkened sky held a sprinkle of stars and a sliver of the moon. The light from the boarding house front porch cast a yellow glow around the yard.

Matthew combed his fingers through his hair. Hollowness gathered inside his body. It was pointless to sleep. He would toss and turn, or worse, dream. It wasn't until he saw Charlie's picture on Lydia's mantle that the nightmares had returned. Matthew had almost erased it from his memory. Could that be why God brought him to this small town? Did he need to come to terms with what he'd done years ago to become the person God wanted?

He plopped down on the sofa and flipped on the television. If he got lucky, he'd find something to take his mind off Charlie Westerman lying on that cold pavement.

It didn't work.

He still smelled the stale beer and rotted pizza that lay throughout that hot Miami alleyway. And visions of large men handcuffed who leaned against cars marked with the agency's emblem. A kid Charlie's age shouldn't have been there, much less dead. He should have been in college or hanging with friends. Not dealing drugs.

He flicked off the set, then pulled out his Bible. Matthew spent the rest of the night reading, looking for some way to find peace for the shooting of an innocent young man.

The next morning, James Newman, III sat in the reception area of the church when Matthew arrived. Beside him slouched a younger replica. His son Jimmy, Matthew assumed. Jimmy's thin face held a few days' growth of hair. His father probably came with him to ensure he kept his appointment. Unfortunately, force usually hurt more than helped in these types of situations.

"Matthew, how are you today?" James rose and pointed toward the younger man. "This is my son, Jimmy."

The younger man's drug addiction showed with his thin body and bad oral care. Most people didn't realize how crack cocaine destroyed not only the inner body, but the outer as well. When most addicts died, they had lost most of their teeth, and their organs had begun to fail.

"It's nice to meet you, Jimmy."

Matthew extended his hand, but Jimmy only gave a slight nod as he sprawled in the chair. His jeans, frayed at the bottom, covered worn tennis shoes.

"Lincolnville Church," Phyllis said, as she answered the telephone a few feet away. "Please hold." She set the receiver on her shoulder and let out a loud sigh. Her morning must have been as bad as Matthew's night. "Matthew, this is Tammy Wiley. She seems real interested in your driving Lydia Frederickson home yesterday evening. She's asking questions about what you two talked about and where her car is. Any suggestions on how you'd like it handled?"

Matthew let out a moan, smoothing his hair. "I'll leave that up to you." Her short tone told him this call had been one of many. That's the problem with a small town. Everyone knew what you did five minutes after you did it.

"Tammy. I believe the pastor doesn't deem his personal life any of my business. Maybe we should plant a bug in his jacket to get exact quotes when he goes out again. After all, there's little else for us to concern ourselves with, is there? I see. Well, it's been nice talking to you, too." A frown crossed over Phyllis as she replaced the receiver on its cradle. "From here on in, I expect an itinerary, and a list of subjects you'll be discussing when you go out with any other single woman in this community. It would save me some trouble in the future."

Matthew let out a loud laugh.

"You were with Lydia last night?" Jimmy slurred his words as he lifted himself from the chair.

"Let's go to my office and make ourselves comfortable?" Matthew pointed the way.

"I'm not about to talk to you." Jimmy spun sharply toward his father before returning a glare to Matthew. "You leave her alone. She deserves better than you." He jerked around Matthew and stormed out.

"I'm sorry." Matthew knew it wasn't his fault but felt an apology would soften any hard feelings. Jimmy'd been looking for an excuse to leave, and he'd found it.

"I'll bet you are." James' expression remained cold. "Certain members of our flock won't appreciate you coming on to the single women in this community so soon after arriving."

Matthew disliked the way James always used the word flock. It was old-fashioned and Pharisee-like. The way he pronounced it gave an added haughty air to his already egotistical disposition.

"If you must know," Matthew said through gritted teeth. "Ms. Frederickson's car broke down on the interstate. I'm not about to leave her sitting alone by the side of the road where who knows what could happen." Matthew worked to contain his anger. "Second, I try not to listen to what a bunch of gossips have to say."

"Let me make myself clear," James said. "You weren't my first choice for pastor. I understand Ms. Frederickson is beautiful, but that's no reason to lose your perspective on things."

Matthew fought the urge to sock the man in the jaw. "I have not lost my perspective. I told you merely seconds ago, the woman's car broke down, and I happened by. We had it towed to my brother-in-law's shop, and I invited her out for a bite." He twisted over his shoulder toward Phyllis. "In case you're asked, she had a ham and cheese sandwich, and I had a burger."

Returning to James, Matthew continued. "When we were told it wouldn't be ready until the next day, I offered her a ride, which she graciously accepted. I'm not sure why I feel the need to explain *again*, but there it is. I would have done the same if you'd been sitting out on the interstate." He chose not to say aloud that he found her more captivating.

"How nice of you." James' jowls went red. "I wouldn't want you accused of doing something you aren't. You have plenty of time to date whatever single woman you chose. I would hate for gossip to be the cause of you losing this job." He adjusted his suit coat as he stomped out.

Matthew's mouth stood opened as the door closed behind James.

Speaking of arrogant. Maybe Lydia should give the sermon this week. Obviously, there were others beside himself who would benefit from a lecture on haughtiness.

"James is just a stubborn old mule," Phyllis said." He thinks if Lydia becomes involved with his little Jimmy, it'll fix all his problems. Sometimes I wonder if he's not the one attracted to her himself." She stood behind Matthew's shoulder as he watched James climb into his car. "So'd you two kiss?"

"Excuse me." Matthew spun.

"You're awful jumpy this morning. Listen, Lydia's a wonderful person, pretty, and you're not bad looking yourself. You're both decent people. You two wouldn't make too bad of a couple." The phone bellowed again. She paused as she walked over to the desk to answer it. "You did say ham and cheese, and a burger, right?"

A smile inched over his lips at Phyllis' approval. It meant a lot to Matthew.

"Hello. Hold on." Phyllis placed the receiver back in its cradle. "It's Riley Owens. What'd you do now? Everyone will probably be calling for an update." She winked.

"I'll take it in my office." Strolling into the back, he reclined in his chair, placing his feet atop the oak desk. If Riley was calling to tease about Lydia, he decided he'd at least be comfortable. "Hello Riley, how are you today?"

"I'm doing okay. You said you drove Lydia back from Ringgold?"

"Yes, I did," Matthew said with a sharp tone. "I hear it'll be on the local news before we know it. Let me guess, we broke a bunch of laws by being seen together."

"Gossip hounds are out this morning, huh?" Riley was all serious. But then he usually was. "I wouldn't be bothering you, but Lydia had a message on her answering machine when she returned last night. It's not a veiled threat anymore."

Matthew bound to his feet. "Is she all right?"

"She's fine. I'm at the house now," Riley said. "I'm hoping you might have caught something this time or seen someone following you two. Think it over, and I'll stop by in a bit, give you time to consider if there was anything or, better yet, anyone that stood out or was out of place."

"You weren't able to retrieve the return number?"

"It came back as long distance. When I tried it, the number was no longer in service. Whoever this is, he knows what he's doing."

"Worse yet, he knows what we're doing." Matthew stared at the panoramic view from his window. "Maybe I should go over."

Matthew wondered if Jimmy had any knowledge about cars.

"I suggest you give it a day or two for things to die down a bit. Besides, Sheryl and Warren are with her now. I'll see you later."

Matthew's midsection tugged as he hung up the telephone. As much as he longed to go to her, Riley was right. He went over in his mind the instances he was with her. The day she dropped off the books, she wore a green blouse and blue jeans. There had been no one lurking about. But then again, he had his attention diverted by the lovely woman he'd been with.

Yesterday she wore a pair of black slacks, and a perfectly fitted beige blouse which caused her eye color to stand out more than usual. Nothing out of the ordinary struck him. Even if there had been, he wouldn't have noticed. It never dawned on him to watch for someone spying on them. He would remedy that from this day forward.

He walked into the sanctuary and stared up at the cross.

"Father, please help Lydia. Help us discover who is terrorizing her. Until we do, please keep her safe." He paused and slid into the nearest pew. His eyes faced the floor. "And God, please help me regarding Charlie Westerman. Le me know the right time to tell her I'm the person who shot her brother. And then help me live with the repercussions."

LYDIA CLENCHED HER jaw tightly, willing herself not to cry as Riley asked her questions about the day.

"Sorry, none of the techs were available last night to take the machine." Riley supervised as an investigator unplugged and packed up the answering machine to take it back to the lab.

"It's all right." A pang of unease came over her at having to explain her walk and then dinner with Matthew. Not that having dinner with Matthew was wrong, Lydia reasoned. It was just somewhat uncomfortable to talk to her husband's close friend about it.

"This guy must have been watching you. Did you recognize anyone familiar?"

"No. Someone could have driven by without me paying particular attention." Lydia squeezed her eyes shut, halting tears from escaping. Matthew had distracted her from paying attention to anything else. "Why did the caller make it sound like I'm having an affair?"

"You aren't cheating, so chase that from your head," Riley said. "Justin would want you to meet somebody who makes you happy. He wouldn't like you taking refuge in this house, not living your life."

"My car broke down, and he drove me home. That's all there was to it."

"This person is affecting your life by making you feel guilty for something you haven't done. Everyone knows how much you and Justin cared for each other. But there comes a time when you have to let go." Riley walked to the front door. He stopped and picked up the picture of Justin from the end table. "Maybe put some of these photographs in a scrapbook. Keep them for memories. You have this placed decorated like a museum, in remembrance of the great Justin Frederickson. He'd be the first to declare he wasn't that great, so pack them away."

"What if I forget him?" Lydia trembled at the thought. "Some days it's hard."

"You won't forget him. The reason it's hard is that you have all these memories staring at you." Riley replaced the photograph. "Take this from a friend of his, remove some of the memorabilia, and redecorate this place. Not only for your health, but for your sanity as well."

"Matthew does seem nice." Lydia lowered her tone.

Riley placed his arm over her shoulder. "This might be hard to imagine, but he is."

His words eased some of the discomfort she carried inside.

"Will you be able to find out who's doing this to her?" Warren said. "Obviously he's following her. We can only imagine what he'll do next." He came up behind them. His lips pierced tight, and his breathing shallow.

A shudder quickly overtook the peace that drew upon Lydia only seconds earlier.

"I'm taking the machine to the lab, and hopefully they can figure something out," Riley responded.

"Maybe if I ask a few questions," Sheryl said, standing beside Warren. "Discreetly, of course. Maybe someone will say something that could help."

"Stirring up a bunch of unwanted dirt on other people won't do any good." Riley shot her a stern look. "You stay here and be a friend."

Sheryl pushed her lip out into her usual teasing pout.

"I can see it now, all the gossips banding together, trying to figure out who's making prank calls to Lydia." Warren rolled his eyes. "By tomorrow, everyone will know the pastor delivered you to your front door. Of course, with this bunch, they'll have you married and with child."

Lydia laughed as she hugged Warren's neck. "How will I survive without you? Whenever things are bad, you're there to make me laugh."

"You'll be fine, Lydia." Riley placed his hand on the small of her back. "Call me, anytime. Sheryl, I do have a job for you."

"Goody, what's that?" Sheryl gushed, clapping her hands.

"Use those art skills of yours and assist the lady in redecorating this house. Lighten it up a little. It feels like a cave in here. Also, try to talk her into removing those rings."

A lump rose in Lydia's throat as she stared down at the one true symbol of her life with Justin.

"And remember, call if anything happens, no matter what time," Riley ordered.

"I will, and don't worry, I'll be fine." Lydia forced a smile, then turned to her two friends. "Let's retreat to the kitchen for those wonderful muffins Warren brought this morning."

"Sounds great. I'm starving." Sheryl pushed Warren toward the kitchen.

"I have no intention of going to Seattle right now." Warren plopped himself down on a chair.

Lydia placed an apple-cinnamon muffin on a plate for each of them. "It's the job you've always dreamed of."

"And teens could use some clean video games to play," Sheryl added.

"It doesn't matter." Warren pushed his muffin toward the center of the table. His lips puckered as he stared down.

"Why not?" Sheryl placed her hand on Warren's arm. "Are you nervous about the job?"

"It's not that. I'm not about to leave with Lydia being threatened. If something happened once I left, I'd never get over it." Warren toyed with his fork.

"You would feel bad if you stayed and something happened to her," Sheryl said.

"I can't leave when some guy is out there preparing to do God knows what."

All this talk about what could happen next caused Lydia unease, but she forced her voice to remain even. "I won't hear another word about it." Lydia took Warren's hand in hers. "You're not going to allow this creep to stop you from living your life. This is a job of a lifetime, and you should take it. As much as I'll miss you, it'll be good for you to go. I couldn't be prouder."

"Besides, Ms. Right could be waiting there for you to arrive." Sheryl smiled. "If you stay, you'll miss out on meeting her."

"My days of meeting Ms. Right have passed by." Warren stuffed the last portion of muffin into his mouth.

"Well, with Seattle being so liberal, maybe you'll meet Mr. Right." Sheryl giggled.

Warren bumped her with his elbow. "I'm afraid I don't swing that way."

"We'll stay in touch by phone and computer, so if anything happens, you'll know." Lydia hated the thought of him losing such a golden opportunity because of her.

"Yeah. And it'll give us somewhere new to vacation." Sheryl beamed. "I'm so proud of you, too. I'll bet you'll be running the company before you know it."

"I doubt that, but I'll mull it over," Warren said.

"Good. Now let's get down to the real business." Sheryl grinned. "Give us the scoop on the evening with the hunky new pastor."

MATTHEW STRETCHED HIS neck as he pulled in front of Anna's. Riley was leaning against the hood of the tan sheriff's car, his shoulders slumped. Matthew invited him in, but he declined.

"I still have some paperwork to do. Sorry I'm late. There was a hit and run off Newberry I had to attend to. In a town this small, no one gets away with anything. Yet two young boys stealing daddy's pickup decided to go for a joyride. Half the block saw them when they sideswiped two cars." He paused before asking, "Did you think of anyone who could have been watching you and Lydia?"

"No, but then again, I didn't look." Matthew noticed Riley's worried expression. "I plan to change that from here on out."

"Probably wouldn't have been easy looking past her anyway," Riley said.

"No, it's hard to detect anything else when she's close by. She's what my daddy calls a breath-taker."

"That she is." Riley half-laughed, yet it did nothing to soften the angles on his face. "Apparently you seem to have gotten her attention, too."

"You don't say" Matthew wanted to jump and kick his heels but decided against it.

"Take it slow, though. She feels she's cheating on Justin by being attracted to you." Riley leaned against his car. "The calls only add to her distress level."

"I can imagine." Matthew propped himself against the cruiser next to Riley. "The worst part is you watch everyone differently than you did before, unsure if they're the person making the calls."

"Spoken from experience?"

"I knew a lady in L.A. whose teenage daughter had been stalked. Creep started by calling, then he began leaving raunchy notes on her car. I followed her, to try to catch the guy. It turned out to be some neighbor older than her mother."

"I imagine you had a talk with him and convinced him to stop."

"Unfortunately, he fell into my fist while we discussed the situation." Matthew leaned toward Riley. "It happened a few years before my Christian days."

"He bother her again?"

"Nope."

"I'm worried about the radiator. When I told her, she tried to stay strong, but the fear was evident." Riley stared at the ground. "It would be too much of a coincidence not to assume it's the same person."

"I agree." Matthew's jaw tightened. "We've got to catch him before he moves it up another notch." He kicked dirt with the toe of his boot as a smile stole over him. "Especially since she finds me attractive."

"I believe I said you've got her attention, yet I can't figure out why." Riley then added, "Do me a favor. Be careful with her. She's been through a lot."

"I realize that." Matthew knew if he chose to move forward with any type of relationship with Lydia, he would have to take the secret of her brother's death to his grave.

"There isn't a man in this town who wouldn't hope to win her," Riley said. "Even some of the married ones."

Warren's feelings for Lydia hadn't bypassed Matthew. The long-lost stare gave it away. Lydia would only think of him as a friend, nothing more. Of course, Jimmy's reaction earlier showed his feelings also. And Phyllis remarked that James could have an attraction to her as well. A list of suspects rose in Matthew's mind. He caught himself giving Riley a sideways glance.

"Including you?" If Riley told him he cared for her, no matter his feelings, Matthew would step aside if his friend asked him to.

"No. Lydia and I became close friends when her husband was sick. I know she's a special lady, but she's not for me. I would just hate to see her hurt again."

"I have no intention of hurting her." Matthew knew that wasn't true. Once he told her about killing her brother, he'd bring her more pain than she was feeling now. As much as he wanted to keep it secret, he knew she would eventually find out.

"I know. But whoever this guy is, if you're the one who catches her attention, there's a possibility you'd be putting your life in danger. There's no way she could go through that again."

10

Lydia had slept well the night before. No phone call disturbed her. She woke eager to attend church and to see Matthew again. The sun glowed through the windshield as she pulled into the parking lot.

Arctic fingers grabbed her above the wrist as she stepped from her car. She tore away and spun to confront Jimmy Newman standing behind her. His addiction to crack cocaine had taken a terrible toll on what used to be wonderful looks. His once perfect white smile now held spaces between blackened teeth.

"Hello Jimmy." She tried to calm the panic that had risen.

"How are you doing?" The pair of blue jeans he wore hung off his hips, and a faded t-shirt with some band painted on the front hung to mid-thigh. He looked near death with his thin face.

"I'm doing fine."

Sadness filled her for what he'd become. His voice rasped from too many cigarettes. His formerly bright eyes were now dull, round orbs sunk into their sockets.

"Last night I overheard my dad talking about them calls you been getting. It's funny how the people around here are. They seem more concerned with what you and the pastor are doing than somebody scaring you." Concern came into his tone. "But I'm not like them. I care about you. I hate the idea of anybody hurting you."

"Riley's been looking into it. Hopefully, he'll discover who it is."

"If I find him, I'll take care of him for you." An intense look advanced into Jimmy's eyes as the roar of a motorcycle sounded.

Lydia attempted to hide her elation as Matthew pulled up. He made an imposing figure, stepping from the bike, his tight leather jacket covering his torso.

"You're kind of hooked on him, aren't you?"

"He's a nice man, but we haven't known each other long." A frown climbed over Jimmy's face. She didn't mean to hurt him. "What we had when we were kids will always be special to me. I still remember how you looked in your tux for the prom."

"You were the prettiest girl there. All the boys were jealous 'cause you came with me. You're still the prettiest girl. There's no way I could win you now. I'm just a bum."

She patted his forearm. "Focus on yourself and stay off those drugs. That's where your attention needs to be."

Every time she saw Jimmy, it brought up the remembrance of her brother. Charlie was the person who got Jimmy hooked. Lydia recalled the first time she caught him selling to Jimmy. She threatened to go to the sheriff. Charlie left town that night, then ended up dead. Guilt floated through Lydia for chasing her brother away.

"Lydia." Matthew walked up behind them. "Jimmy, please join us for the service?"

"I ain't gonna listen to your preaching." Jimmy lifted the side of his lip in a sneer. He turned back to Lydia. "He'll never care for you like I do. No one will." He turned and walked away.

Lydia watched Jimmy pick something up from the sidewalk before he crossed the street. He lit a match before he placed the item in his mouth and then caught fire to it.

Matthew held her by the arm, a distressed look in his eyes. Could he be as worried about Jimmy as she was?

"It's sad. He used to be the most popular kid in school. Now look at him." Before Lydia entered the church building, she turned and watched Jimmy wander away from them and God.

THE WHISPERS BEGAN as soon as they entered the sanctuary together. Murmurs continued even after that morning's sermon on gossip.

"Lydia." James Newman, III crossed the aisle and sat beside her after the service. "I saw you talking with Jimmy before you got interrupted." His jaw was taught as he glanced in Matthew's direction.

"He looks pretty frail," she whispered.

"How about joining us for lunch? You two kids can get reacquainted."

"Are you ready?" Sheryl passed Lydia a gray shawl. "Riley says he'll meet us at the house."

"Riley? Are you having more problems?" James glanced between the two women.

"No. We're having a small gathering of friends," Lydia explained. "They're worried I'll rust spending all my time in my house."

"And guess who else I've invited?" Sheryl grinned. "Matthew. He's agreed to join us."

"You've gone through a rough period," James said. "And you deserve a decent man in your life. However, people are already talking about you and Matthew." He leaned closer and whispered. "It's not pleasant what they're saying."

"I'm not really interested in what a bunch of nosey people are saying." Lydia tried to control her curt tone as she rose from the pew. "It's really no one's business."

"You have a wonderful reputation," James said as he stood. "I wouldn't want a bunch of rumors to ruin that. Also, with the minister being new here, it isn't acceptable for him either."

"Lydia's reputation will do fine." Matthew stopped behind James. "And if a bunch of cackling old hens are enough for me to lose my job, then it wasn't God's will I have it."

"I'm just warning you." James snapped. He reeled around Matthew and stormed out.

MATTHEW LEFT WITHIN thirty minutes of Lydia. He couldn't believe how enthusiastic he was to see her again. No matter how hard he fought it, he cared for her. If he were smart, he'd head home and not steer toward those that could read right through him. Seeing Jimmy earlier reminded him of Charlie, and how the young man never got the chance to get his life together.

Matthew hesitated and looked over the neatly aligned hedges of Sheryl's home. He tugged off his helmet and stood. "I really like playing with fire, don't I?"

"Matthew, welcome." Sheryl led him into the house. "Lydia's out back."

"What makes you think it's only Lydia I came to see?"

"Because when I mentioned her name, I saw the vein of your neck throb."

Out on the covered patio, Lydia, Warren, Riley, and Wendy Moreland laughed and talked with one another. Sheryl must have decided to play matchmaker for everyone, including herself.

After Matthew greeted the other guests, he found a seat next to Riley. He couldn't pull his attention from Lydia as she leaned on the railing. Her shoes sat on the concrete floor beside her. She wore a forest green dress and commanded attention without even trying. A silver wrap covered her shoulders as a light breeze cooled the air.

He licked his lips looking at the fried chicken, coleslaw, baked beans and rolls. After eating, as Matthew rinsed his plate in the kitchen sink, he noticed Lydia leaning against a rail, staring over the yard. He walked out and joined her.

"Mind if I join you?" A light hint of vanilla came from her direction. He sucked in the new fragrance. "You smell amazing."

"Thank you."

"When I saw you with Jimmy, I was afraid he'd hurt you." He chose not to tell her. He had concerns Jimmy might be her stalker. Once closer, I realized you were just talking, and he had no intention of doing you any harm. I didn't mean to intrude."

"You didn't. I know he has to fix himself. No one can do it for him. No matter what his father seems to think."

"I gather he believes you could be his son's savior." Matthew leaned back against the railing.

"He hated it when we broke up."

Matthew leaned in as she spoke. He waited for her to continue.

"We went out in high school, dances, driving around, teen stuff. After the senior prom, he drank quite a bit, and we were in an accident."

Matthew straightened as she talked. Her being injured, even years earlier, bothered him.

"I told him I wouldn't continue to go with him unless he got his act together." She paused. "I wasn't hurt, but my dad was furious about me having to be driven home by a deputy. If Jimmy hadn't been in jail, my dad probably would have killed him."

"And Jimmy didn't get his act together." Matthew moved a strand of hair that had blown across her forehead. His urge to kiss her grew. *God*, he silently prayed, *give me strength not to take Lydia in my arms. Unless, of course, it's Your will.*

"In fact, not even a week later, he found himself in jail for burglary and drug possession. He received six years, was out in half that. While out on bail, he came to see me. I told him I was leaving for college and wouldn't be seeing him again. He went to prison, and I got married. Unfortunately, James has it in his head that his son and I are the perfect couple. He doesn't seem to realize it was a high school thing."

Matthew stood beside her, looking over the yard in silence. It felt natural to Matthew, being with this woman, comfortable enough not to speak.

"Maybe I'm just trying to get him to quit because my brother's the one who first got him to do drugs."

Matthew's pulse raced at the mention of Charlie. "Jimmy's a grown man. He needs to take responsibility for his actions." A voice in Matthew's head laughed and said, *"Like you?"*

"Do you suppose he'll ever recover?" She looked at him with pleading eyes. Matthew wished he could assure her of Jimmy's recovery, but he knew the odds were against it.

"As long as he's willing, there's always hope." He pulled her into a one-armed hug. "A dad hoping to fix him up with some old girlfriend won't do him any good. Prayer will. God can turn his spirit, so he'll want to recover." Matthew then thought to himself, if the drugs don't cut his life short.

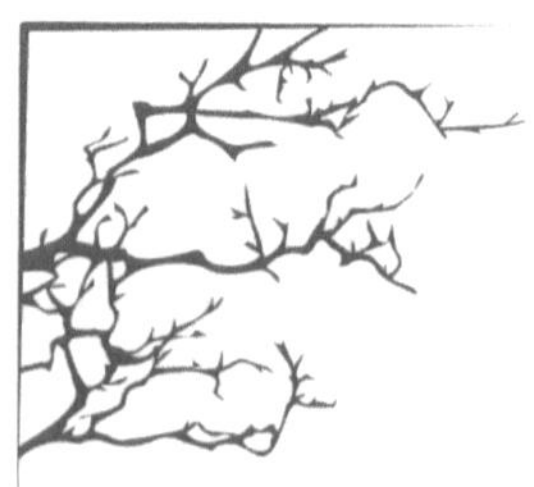

11

"Hello." Lydia woke from a sound sleep. "Hello," she spoke into the phone. Again, concern for her parents forced her to pick up the ringing telephone.

"Cheating on Justin. Tsk. Tsk."

Lydia slammed down the telephone. She wasn't cheating. Justin was dead. *God, please help me. Let me know whether it's time to move on.* Was it God's plan to put Matthew in her life? She rolled over and did her best to fall back to sleep.

After tossing and turning for most of the night, she woke and poured herself a cup of coffee. The morning sun lifted over the horizon on that Saturday. It was just after seven when she tossed her purse over her shoulder and headed out the door. Cool air cut through her sweater as she marched to the cemetery. Once there, she bent in front of Justin's stone.

"My darling, why did you have to die? Things would be so much easier if you hadn't left." She touched his name. "I've met someone. It's not serious, at least not yet. But it could be, maybe in time." She brushed at a tear. "I think it's time to move on with my life. Not that I'll forget you, I couldn't. But I feel like I'm choking inside from the guilt. I feel it's time to let go."

Lydia sat on the damp grass as she recalled her life with Justin. She continued to talk to the stone. She cried about her loss, laughed about the time they spent with each other. The heat from the sun warmed her skin as it rose in the blue sky.

"I miss you, and I always will." She kissed her hand and again placed her palm against his name. The diamond from her engagement ring

94

glistened in the sun. She kissed the wedding ring set, then removed them and placed them in her sweater pocket. The binding that choked her heart fell, giving room to move forward with her life, whether it be with Matthew or someone else. She sucked in a deep breath. The air felt fresh and new.

As she rose to her feet, she realized Jimmy Newman watched from the other side of the street. It gave her an eerie sensation, having been unaware of his presence. Twice now he'd appeared from nowhere. Could he be the person calling her? Caution weighed heavy as she walked in his direction. She studied the surrounding area for anyone else lurking about before she stepped from the curb.

"Jimmy, how are you?"

He reminded her of the old saying, "rode hard and put up wet." He wore a pair of faded jeans with holes, and a sour aroma filtered from him. His unkempt hair appeared in dire need of washing.

"I'm okay." Jimmy shoved his hands to the bottom of his pockets. "Can I ask you something?" He added, "Personal."

"I guess."

"There ain't no way we'll ever get back together, is there?" He stared at the cement sidewalk.

"No, Jimmy. We had our moment," Lydia responded. "We both moved on. Think about rehab and nothing else right now. After you're through, then you can focus on getting yourself a wife who'll treat you the way you deserve."

"I always assumed it'd be you."

"I'm sorry. Who's to say, even without the other stuff, whether we'd have gotten married or not." She touched his forearm. "We were kids. People change when they get older."

He lowered his head. "It's okay. I know I'm a loser."

She swallowed hard. She hated how he saw himself. "Jimmy, that's not what it is."

"I understand." He turned to go but paused. "I hope you have a great life, Lydia. You deserve it."

She wondered how Jimmy's life would be different if he had abstained from taking his first taste of drugs. Would he have gone on to a football career or become the doctor he'd once dreamed of being? Anger rose toward Charlie for getting Jimmy hooked. Her brother hadn't stopped at ruining his own life, he had to ruin others' lives as well. Hard telling how many more people than Jimmy he got hooked by his destructive behavior.

The rings lining her pocket bounced against her side as she strolled down the sidewalk. She contemplated Jimmy's words and agreed. She did deserve to have a great life. Instead of turning south on Devonshire to her home, Lydia headed west on Wilson. She bought a bouquet of flowers from a local nursery.

As she approached the corner, the large, elegant mansion of Anna's Boarding House blocked the sun. A long porch encircled the magnificent brick house. Six rocking chairs aligned the front, and a round wrought-iron table stood between each pair.

Lydia had to force her mouth to close when she saw Matthew. He wore a pair of jeans and a sleeveless tank top as he worked on his motorcycle. He made a striking picture.

Anna Richmond, the owner of the building where he lived, stood over him. Her plump frame wiggled as she used her hands to relate some tale. Her orange hair stood upright in a pointed mess as gray snuck through at the roots. Matthew would turn his head every few seconds, giving her attention while he worked on his bike.

As Lydia closed within feet, the full image of the tattoo appeared on Matthew's arm. The snake draped over a cross with vines surrounding both. She wondered how long it took to do such an intricate illustration. A barbed wire tattoo encircled the other bicep. His sleeve had hidden the tattoo until now.

She gawked at the muscles in his upper arms as he bent, using a socket wrench near his rear wheel. His powerfully built arms glistened with perspiration. The white tank top stretched, tightening with each breath of air.

Her stomach did a somersault as those piercing blue eyes caught sight of her. She rearranged her hair, fighting the urge to run into his arms.

MATTHEW ROSE AS LYDIA neared. Everything fit her to a tee, from the dark pair of blue jeans to the button-down blouse covered with a pink sweater. The complete outfit accentuated her curves. Curves he struggled to ignore whenever he saw her. He wished God had given him a warning of her presence. He tugged the greasy tank top from his sweaty body.

"Well, I'll be." Ms. Richmond walked toward Lydia and gave her a peck on the cheek. "If it's not Ms. Lydia Frederickson out and about so early this morning." Ms. Richmond's accent proved her to be a proper Southern Belle. "I was going to fetch myself a cup of coffee. Would y'all care for some?"

"No, thank you. I only stopped by for a moment." Lydia sniffed the bouquet.

"Well, I'd best be leaving. I have a wild idea it's not me you've come to visit." She smiled and squeezed Lydia's arm. "Y'all enjoy the day now, ya hear."

"You, too." Lydia handed Matthew the bouquet. "These are for you."

"For me. Why?" He accepted the flowers, puzzled by her actions. When the scent of gardenia surrounded him, he practically melted into a puddle on the ground. It reminded him of when he first bumped into her at Fred's Diner. The aroma swept through his dreams at night.

"For helping when my car broke down. I really appreciated it, and they're to say thank you."

He glimpsed at the arrangement. "I can honestly say I've never received flowers before." It showed how she differed from other women.

Lydia grinned as she skimmed the leather bike seat with her hand. "I'm glad I'm the first."

Matthew noticed the wedding ring set had disappeared from her hand. He decided not to bring it up for fear the reason might not be him. "They smell wonderful," he said.

"It's a wonderful day to discover new things and new people." She cocked her head with a glint in her eye.

His mind spun in a million different directions. He tried to rein in his excitement so as not to appear eager as he tried to contemplate her words. That voice inside his head shouted, "*Tell her about Charlie before it's too late.*" He again ignored it.

"I mulled over what you said the other day by the side of the road about getting to know each other. I'd like to try it" She hesitated. "As long as it is slow."

"I'll let you set the pace." He longed to grab her and plant a kiss on those luscious lips. He resisted, aware *that* wasn't moving slow. "How about we do dinner this evening? An official first date?"

"Okay."

A shade of pink gathered in her cheeks from the crisp air. Matthew had to remind himself to inhale as he stared.

"How about I pick you up at seven?" he said.

"I'll be ready." After she had walked a few feet, she stopped and turned. "Where are we going? I want to wear the proper attire." She gave him a big smile.

"How about we keep it casual? Some place simple, not too formal." He moved to the other side of the motorcycle and leaned against it. "What you're wearing now will suffice."

"If you say so." Her eyes sparkled. "I'll see you at seven."

His heart hovered behind her as she sauntered away.

Matthew showered after Lydia left. It would have been pointless to go on working when all he wanted to do was follow her like a stray dog. She could scratch him behind the ears any day.

He laughed at the notion. Within minutes, he pulled up to her house. He hoped he wasn't too early, but he'd been anxious all day to see her again. He had pushed any thought of Charlie Westerman from his mind.

Lydia had changed into a peach-colored turtle-neck sweater. She'd pulled her hair up, leaving a few strands loose that gave softness to her face. It took every ounce of energy for Matthew's heart to keep from jumping out his throat.

"So, where are we going?"

"I thought Fred's Diner would be the perfect place." Matthew choked out the words.

"Fred's?"

"Well, it really is *our* place where we first met." Did he catch a hint of disappointment? "If you'd rather go somewhere else, I'll be happy to oblige."

"No, Fred's will be fine." She stopped when she saw the motorcycle. "How about we take my car? I'll even let you drive." She held up the keys.

"If you insist." He smiled at her while inwardly upset for suggesting the local diner. There were plenty of nicer restaurants nearby. He assumed he'd already blown it, and the evening hadn't even started.

GOING TO FRED'S DINER let off a lot of the pressure. It reeked casual and comfortable. Lydia hoped her inner being stopped jumping up and down. The acrobats had been busy since she arrived home.

She climbed into the passenger side of the Civic as Matthew held the door open. Once in the driver's seat, he barely had room to move.

"There's a knob on the side to move the seat or make it recline a bit." Lydia leaned over to show him. The spicy core with the leathery background of his cologne inched into her nostrils. When she glimpsed his blue eyes, her heart throbbed. She returned upright and pulled open the vanity mirror and ran her fingers through her hair. She pictured her heart thumping through her sweater.

Matthew winked at her in the mirror as a blush traveled from her forehead to her neck. He lifted her hand and kissed the back of it. A fiery sensation voyaged through her. His masculine fingers enveloped hers as he drove. The warmth seeped in deep. Her nerves were jumpy, like when she had her first date as a teenager. *Please, Lord, don't let me ruin it.*

Within five minutes, Matthew pulled the car into a parking space behind the building housing Fred's. As they entered, the smell of burnt grease assaulted them.

"I believe they kept that burger on longer than necessary." Lydia covered her nose as she marched to a booth farthest from the grill.

"That would be my burger." Matthew laughed. "What can I say? I take them well done."

"That's not well done. That's ashen."

"Hello, Pastor. How are you today?" Dolly brought over two cardboard menus.

"I'm doing fine, Dolly. I'll take a BLT and root beer." Matthew returned the menu to her.

"And the lady?" Dolly looked down at Lydia with a grin.

"Hello Dolly. How're the kids?" Lydia gave her a smile.

"Growing big and full of trouble."

"I imagine. I'll have the chef's salad with a glass of water." Lydia leaned across the table toward Matthew once Dolly retreated. "You can hear the arteries hardening in here, can't you?"

"I'm shocked to catch you here." Warren surprised Lydia by appearing behind her. "Are you telling me the preacher has dispelled all your healthy eating habits? Matthew, glad to see you again before I leave."

"You, too." He glanced at Warren, then returned his attention to Lydia.

"I'm coming in to catch a quick bite," Warren said. "I've finished packing and will stop by before I ride off into the sunset tomorrow afternoon. So, what brings you to Fred's?"

Lydia looked up with a grin. "Warren, we're on a date."

"A date. Here?" Warren laughed as he patted Matthew on the shoulder. "I'm not a lady's man by any means, but I've read enough books on the proper places to take one on a date. I don't recall the local greasy spoon being mentioned."

A smug look seeped across Warren's face. It wasn't like him to be pompous. Lydia hoped it wasn't because of his new job. If getting this position in Seattle meant his ego would inflate, he'd be better off not having it.

"I would appreciate any ideas you can give me for the future." Matthew winked at Lydia.

As she looked away from the two men, a rush of heat fell across her cheeks.

"I'm surprised Sheryl hasn't called with the news." Warren then whispered, "She's always up on the gossip."

"I haven't told her." Lydia said. "Why bother getting her hopeful if it doesn't work out?"

"She'll be sorely disappointed she missed this." Warren placed his hand to the side of his mouth. "I'll make a point of telling her so she's fully aware."

"You're too funny." Lydia wondered how Matthew felt about all the gossip that went on in this little town. She worried he would reconsider asking her out again.

"Well, you two enjoy the rest of your evening." Warren gave a smirk in Matthew's direction. "And Matthew, we really need to meet about the finer places to take a lady."

Matthew let out a loud laugh. It caused some of Lydia's apprehension to leave.

Left alone again, Lydia stared at Matthew, who gave off a look that was warm and inviting in a way she hadn't noticed before. She wondered how her knees had weakened; after all, she was sitting down. The evening continued with interruptions by people stopping to say their hellos. As the intruders took their seats, they would stare and whisper. Their date would be all over the grapevine within an hour.

After dinner, Matthew drove the car toward Devonshire. "I guess I should have spoken to Warren before deciding on a place. He'd have suggested somewhere more private."

"I had a wonderful evening."

"Even with all the stares?" Matthew's jaw set tight, and his mouth formed a frown.

"Let them look. They're jealous because my escort happens to be the most eligible bachelor in the area." She touched his arm. The warmth of his skin came through the sleeve.

Matthew laughed again. His jaw relaxed, and the tension left his face as he took her hand.

Her heart did a flip when they pulled up in front of her house. Were the rules different for dating a minister than a regular guy? What would be the appropriate protocol? Her insides shook as he escorted her by the elbow to the front door.

"I hope you did enjoy yourself. I probably should have taken you somewhere other than Fred's." Matthew ran his knuckle under her chin.

"I had a wonderful evening." Butterflies flew constantly inside.

"I hoped to get to know you better. Less interruptions."

"You wanted it informal."

"That I did. Next time, some place a little less busy." Matthew faced the ground. "If you allow a next time."

She grinned. "I believe I can do that."

He touched her hair, and her midsection shuddered. If he tried, would she allow him to kiss her? Disappointment flushed in as he touched his lips to her cheek.

"I guess I'll see you in church tomorrow."

He brushed her lips with his thumb. Tempted to grab it with her teeth, she decided against of it. Proper etiquette probably didn't include biting a minister, in any religion.

"I'll be there." Lydia hoped she sounded indifferent instead of frustrated. Once inside the house, her shoulders released. She hadn't realized how tense she'd been. If he had kissed her, she probably would have fainted in his arms.

She chose not to answer the telephone that buzzed as she entered the bedroom. She didn't want to take the chance on someone destroying her evening. Within seconds, her cell rang. The caller ID read Winters, M.

A grin crawled onto her lips as she answered.

"I called your home number a moment ago, but there was no answer." Matthew's deep voice came over the line. "I got a bit worried."

"I'm fine. I've unplugged it so I can get a restful night's sleep."

"Sounds like a wonderful idea. I called to say goodnight."

"Goodnight."

The motorcycle engine roared, then faded into the dark. Lydia smiled. She placed her hand against her heart and admitted it to herself. She actually felt happy.

12

Lydia spun the tomato, looking for any imperfections before placing it in the green basket she carried. The bright overhead lights cast a glare on the perfectly aligned apples in a variety of green, red, and yellow. After having placed two Red Delicious apples in her basket, she walked over to the cantaloupe. A spicy smell drifted over her. Matthew. Her pulse jumped, declaring feelings she couldn't ignore. It had been three days since their date at Fred's, and Lydia could think of nothing else.

"Are you following me?" She spoke without turning around.

"You need to eat more meat." He looped his arm over her shoulder. "There's absolutely nothing fattening in here. No chocolate to put some padding on those bones."

She elbowed him in the ribs, and he flinched. "I have enough padding, thank you very much."

"There are too many fruits and vegetables. There isn't one thing in there that isn't healthy. Live a little."

"I live just fine. Besides, I'm here with Warren. He's decided to fly out so he could stay a few extra days. He's picking up the bad stuff."

"Great. You had me worried there for a minute." Matthew leaned against the produce counter. "Is Warren excited about his new job?"

"I think so. A mixture of euphoria and nervousness. Especially since he's going to a new place that he's unfamiliar with and has no friends or family." Lydia frowned. She already missed him, and he hadn't left yet.

"I gave him the number to my pastor friend who has yet to meet a stranger. Warren should have no trouble. He's also agreed to allow

Warren to stay in his spare room until he finds a place of his own." Matthew glanced at his watch. "I guess I'll see you later. I have a meeting at 11:30. You are coming to the service on Wednesday, aren't you?"

"I'll be there."

"And how about dinner Friday?" A look of apprehension crawled over him.

She smiled. "What shall I wear?"

"Something nice." Matthew leaned toward her. "I plan to take Warren's advice and take you somewhere more appropriate."

Lydia laughed as she watched Matthew amble off.

"Boo!"

Lydia jumped. Jimmy Newman's arms enclosed her waist. He swung her, taking her feet off the ground. "I seen you talking to your preacher. You really like him, don't you?"

"He's nice enough." Lydia struggled to pull away, but Jimmy's hold tightened. He reeked of alcohol. She assumed he'd also started taking drugs again.

"I can be real nice, too." He whispered loudly into her ear. "How about I show you how nice I can be?"

"Jimmy. I need to get a few more things before Warren's ready to go."

"Warren, huh? You think so much of him. I could tell you stories." He released his hold and grabbed a banana, peeled it back, and ate it. He tossed the peel back in the bin with the other uneaten fruit. "Come on Lydia. I remember how much fun we used to have. Take a walk with me."

"I can't, I'm busy."

"Come on. Your preacher won't need to know."

"Jimmy, please stop it." Unease crept in at the fact he seemed to be following her.

"I'm only asking you to go for a walk." His voice tensed as he grabbed her by the wrist. Her basket toppled onto the floor. Its contents scattered across the aisle. "I ain't asking you to marry me. Let's go find a nice place where we can be alone. You used to enjoy being alone with me."

Pain shot up her arm. "Jimmy stop. You're hurting me." Hands grabbed him by the scruff of the neck. He winced.

"Let go of the lady before I break you in two." Matthew's look told Lydia he meant business.

Jimmy quickly released her, yet Matthew continued his hold. Warren stood behind the two men, anger hanging over him as well. Other customers gathered also. Lydia hated all the attention it was garnering.

Jimmy finally freed himself. "You ain't got no right to touch me," he shouted.

"You leave her alone, and I won't have to touch you." Inches separated the two men.

"I'll see to it my dad has you fired, preacher man." Jimmy retreated, bumping into a nearby produce stand, sending oranges rolling to the floor. He stumbled upright before running out the rear of the store.

"Did he hurt you?" Warren walked up to Lydia, his lips thin as anger reigned in his eyes.

Lydia could hardly retrieve her senses. "Maybe my arm."

Matthew moved Lydia's wrist, not saying a word or making an indication he noticed the bruising beginning to show. "Let's get you to a doctor to have it looked at." He then pulled her into a hug.

She clung to him as tears escaped. "He was drunk." She ached at Jimmy falling off the wagon again. She'd hoped he would finally break the addiction.

"Let's take you to Dr. Reese." Warren guided her to the car with Matthew on her other side. "Don't worry. I'll take care of you."

"How about I call Riley?" Matthew said as he helped her to the car. "He could pick Jimmy up and put him in a cell. Even if it's overnight, it would give him a chance to sober up and realize what he's done."

"Or give him more of a reason to drink," Lydia said as Matthew opened the door for her. "I'll be fine, and you've got a meeting to get to."

"I can postpone it." He touched the side of her cheek. "You're my top priority."

His words made Lydia feel safe and warm. "I'll be fine. Besides, Warren will take care of me. If you think Sheryl's a mother hen, you've not seen anything until Warren takes over."

"If you insist." Matthew looked over Lydia's shoulder at Warren. "Do me a favor and stay close to her until you get her home. We can't be too sure where Jimmy wandered off to."

Warren scanned the parking lot, his jaw still taut.

She hated to cause of all this tension.

At the doctor's office, Dr. Reese placed Lydia's sprained wrist in a brace to be worn for a week. It took Lydia over an hour to get Warren to leave once she got home. Her heart skipped a beat when her cell phone rang. A dash of disappointment wandered in upon seeing it wasn't Matthew.

"Hello Riley," she said. "I'm assuming someone called you about Jimmy."

"Are you all right?" His voice carried the concern she knew it would. He had to be getting tired of taking care of her.

"I've got a sprain, but I'll be fine."

"If you want to file a complaint, I'll pick him up. Wouldn't hurt him to sit in jail for a day or two."

"But it might hurt his mother, Melanie. She's been through and he's been in jail before with no luck, so there's really no point in doing it again."

"He could be your stalker."

"But there's no way to be sure. And I'd hate to hurt his family if it turns out we're wrong. Besides, he's never come after me before. Why would he now?"

"Drugs make you do bad things," Riley said. "If you change your mind, just say so."

Once she hung up, she looked at the ceiling. "Please God, don't let Jimmy hurt himself or someone else just because I didn't join him for a walk."

LYDIA CLOSED THE LID to the trash can as the dark blue Lincoln Town Car pulled up to the curb. James and Melanie Newman stepped from the vehicle. Lydia swallowed down her tension as they approached. She hadn't seen them at church on Wednesday, two days ago. Hopefully, they didn't know about her altercation with Jimmy. A lot to hope for in such a small town.

Her stomach was already doing jumps because of her date with Matthew; she didn't need any more anxiety.

"Lydia, how are you?"

James wore the same smile as when he asked for campaign donations. Lydia ran over the date in her mind to see if he might be on the campaign trail.

"I'm doing fine," Lydia said. "How are you two?"

"Not too good." Tears stood in Melanie's eyes. "We haven't heard from Jimmy since Tuesday afternoon."

James added. "He told us what happened at the store."

Lydia just nodded, waiting for one of them to continue.

James leaned in and lowered his voice. "It looks like our pastor might have a bit of a temper on him."

"What are you talking about?" Lydia took a step back.

"Jimmy told me Matthew attacked him just for talking to you," James said.

"And you believed him?" Lydia wanted to attack James at that moment. She looked at Melanie for some response but got none. "It couldn't be that maybe Jimmy was lying to you, could it?"

"Why would he?" James's face carried a stunned look.

"Because he's drinking again." Lydia let out a loud sigh. "He was drunk and tried to drag me from the store. All Matthew did was make him let go."

"I can't believe Jimmy would ever try to hurt you." James' voice held a light tremor. "He's always cared very much for you."

"I don't think he meant to hurt me. He just did." Lydia held up her wrist, revealing the brace. "I'm sorry."

"That explains why we haven't seen him." Melanie took hold of Lydia's hand. "Is it anything serious?"

"No, I'll be fine. I know you hoped this time he'd quit. We all did."

James nodded his head. "He needs a good woman to take care of him. Someone like you."

"No." Lydia let out a weighted breath. "What he needs is to decide to change and ask God to help him. James, neither you nor I can help him if he doesn't want it."

"I suppose you're right." He paused. "I guess I'm just worried about you, that's all."

"Worried about what?" Anxiety crept in.

"Everyone knows about those terrible phone calls. And the women, you know how some of them gossip. Word has gotten around that you're seeing Matthew."

She forced herself not to roll her eyes. Women aren't the only ones who gossip. Lydia chose not to speak the words. Maybe her silence would hurry him to his point so he would move on, and she could get ready for her date. She suppressed a grin as she wondered how James would react if he knew she was seeing Matthew that very night.

"Not that he isn't a great guy, and you have every reason to see him. It's just that some women are saying they saw you making out on your front porch the other night. That's not exactly appropriate behavior for a Christian woman, or a minister, for that matter."

"James!" Melanie gave her husband a harsh look as Lydia's mouth dropped open.

James put his hands up. "Now, what you do is between you and God, but you have to think of the children who may be watching."

Lydia placed her hands on her hips. "I haven't done anything wrong. All he did was kiss me on the cheek. But if we did make out, I bet he'd be good at it," she blurted. "Maybe you'd better stop listening to the gossip yourself and get the whole story."

Riley's cruiser pulled in behind the Newman's automobile. James seemed oblivious to the sheriff's arrival.

"I'm sorry. I should have known. You've never come off like some sort of harlot. Besides, I can't believe you'd treat Justin's memory like that. He was such a good man."

Lydia felt the blood drain from her face as reality crashed in around her. Except for a few quick moments, she hadn't thought about the phone calls. Could James be the one making them? What was it the caller said? Something about treating Justin like that. Sweat beads popped out on her forehead, and her breathing intensified. *Please God, don't let me panic.*

"Lydia, what's wrong?" James grabbed her arm. "I didn't mean to upset you."

"Don't touch me." She jerked her arm away from him.

"Lydia, what's going on?" Riley rushed to her side.

James took another step toward her. "I mentioned Justin, and she went pale. I think she might faint."

"Maybe we should get her inside." Melanie approached Lydia, touching her face as if checking for a fever. "It's just all too much with Jimmy hurting you. And she's right." She glanced at her husband with tight lips. "Her dating Matthew is none of our business. They're both good people and deserve happiness."

Lydia swallowed down hard, shaking off all the people who crowded around her. "Thank you for that, Melanie. I appreciate your support. I'm fine, but I have things I need to do right now, so if you'll all excuse me." She turned, held her head high, walked up her porch and through her front door, leaving Riley to deal with the Newmans. Once inside, she worked to recall the words of her caller. Why would James be the person terrorizing her?

Riley walked into the house. "Do you mind telling me what just happened?" He closed the door behind him. "When I pulled up, I thought you were going to have a heart attack right there on your front lawn."

"I think it might be James calling me." Lydia sat on the edge of her sofa. "He said some of the same things that were on the last message."

"I'll look into it. Don't worry. If it's him, we'll prove it. Are you going to be all right?"

Lydia checked her watch. "I'll be fine. I have other things to think about. Like getting ready for my date." She hopped to her feet and gave Riley a smile.

"A date? I sure hope he does better than the diner down the road." Riley gave her a grin and patted her shoulder.

"He'd better. I'm planning to dress up for this one."

WHY COULDN'T HE DECIDE? Women spent all day trying to pick the perfect outfit to wear, not men. Matthew had been on plenty of dates before. So why was his stomach in knots? He was perfectly fine when he took her to Fred's. How could this date be any more special than their first one? And why couldn't he find something to wear?

He had changed into three different slacks with several shirts and two suits before settling on a charcoal suit with a teal shirt beneath. He even had his hair trimmed to below his collar.

In lieu of driving the motorcycle, Matthew borrowed his father's Ford Taurus. After he rounded the block several times to avoid appearing too eager, at 6:55 he finally stood at Lydia's front door. He hoped the anxiety would dissipate before she answered. The knots had gone from granny to double Englishman with a twist.

When she opened the door, his jaw opened, and his mouth went dry. She wore a bold ruby silk dress with black lace strewn throughout. The design reminded him of stained glass. It crossed from shoulder to shoulder, below her neck with barely there cap sleeves. The fit accentuated her waist, flowing to above her knee, showing off her legs. And what legs they were. The finished outfit included a simple pair of black pumps. Her hair was up on the left side, held by an elegant comb, while the other flowed over her shoulders.

Even with the brace on her wrist, he found her breathtaking. Incredible was the first word that popped into his mind. He drew in extra oxygen to keep from going lightheaded.

"Wow." He uttered.

"I'll take that as a compliment." She lowered her head. Pink creased her cheeks.

"You should. You look wonderful." Why would such a captivating woman want to be with him?

"You, too." She smiled.

All his insecurities washed away with that twinkle in her eye. "These are for you." He passed her a dozen lavender roses he bought on the way over. She buried her face in the blooms, taking in the smell before placing them on the side table.

"They're beautiful," Lydia replied. "Don't lavender roses mean you're falling in love?"

Matthew coughed to hide his embarrassment. "I just, I thought they looked nice." He had asked the clerk about the meaning of the colors. Purple seemed most appropriate for his feelings. "Shall we go?"

Grabbing a black wrap from the side of the sofa, she spun it behind her, placing it over her shoulders. She then secured her arm through the crook of his elbow. As she walked down the porch, she leaned into him. "You had me concerned about the ride. I'm not sure I could stay somewhat modest wearing this dress and riding a motorcycle."

He stared at the fabric clinging above her knees, taking in those wonderful calves. "I'm thinking side-saddle wouldn't have done much good either."

They arrived at the four-star restaurant of Simooms' Haute Cuisine outside Chattanooga just before eight. The atmosphere spoke elegance with the large chandeliers floating overhead. The maître d' led them to their seats. A half-dozen black-vested men stood behind a large, dark wooden bar, waiting to serve patrons.

The light overhead bounced off Lydia's hair, causing it to shine. She wore a modicum amount of makeup, which was unnecessary. She would be beautiful without it. What a perfect specimen of God's work.

Throughout the evening, they laughed and talked. The best part, no interruptions from nosy citizens of Lincolnville.

Resistance was futile as he fought to keep his eyes on the road heading back to Lincolnville. He kept trying to steal a glance at the amazing woman beside him.

"You're staring," she said.

"I can't believe how beautiful you are. Makes me feel out of place."

"You? Mr. Confident. I can't believe you'd ever feel out of place."

He did exude confidence, he always had. He stood straight and walked with a gait that told people he believed in what he did. However, when it came to Lydia, insecurities rushed into him. He felt he had to work to make an impact on her.

"Truthfully, you're the only person who does that to me." He paused with the realization. "You're the first woman I've ever tried to impress."

She leaned slightly toward him. "You've never met a woman you wanted to impress? Someone to change for?"

"Unfortunately, the person I once considered for a lifetime became upset when I did change." Matthew went on to explain. "When I went to the seminary, she couldn't leave fast enough." He glanced at Lydia in the glow of the streetlights and smiled. "I guess it wasn't meant to be."

"I suppose not."

Once they pulled up to the front of her house, he bounced out to open her car door. The butterflies had changed to seagulls when he accompanied her up the steps.

"So, was tonight an improvement on Fred's?" Matthew prayed his anxiety didn't show.

"Did I ever say I wasn't thrilled with our first date? But I will commend Warren on how his advice improved your second choice."

"Tell him thanks for the guidance." He waited as she unlocked the door and flipped the inside light on. His insides trembled when her gaze met his.

"I had a wonderful time. Thank you." Her smoky, airless voice added to his jitters.

Matthew dreamt of drowning in her perfume. "You'll be at the service on Sunday, won't you?"

"Will you miss me if I'm not there?"

"You bet I will." Matthew ran his thumb along her jawline before tucking his index finger under her chin. Easing his palm around her neck, he pulled her to him. Her skin felt soft against his hand. The pulse in her throat drummed against his hand. As their lips met, he swore he heard an explosion of fireworks.

SHE SHOULDN'T HAVE closed her eyes. Then it wouldn't have happened. But she did, and it did. Lydia hovered in space. Had it been only a short while ago her only concern had been some fool making annoying phone calls? At the present, Matthew captivated her thoughts.

When he arrived in that charcoal-colored suit, her mind went totally blank. Any other thoughts vanished instantly. He had even cut his hair to his collar, causing it to curl at the ends. On most men, it would have said safe and controlled, but it gave Matthew a roguish quality.

She remembered feeling dizzy as he gave her the roses. Lavender had been the perfect color. It was too soon for red. The moon glistened overhead, and the stars danced above. Even though cold out, she hadn't noticed. And that kiss. Her heart had yet to slow. Lydia now knew where the phrase "rockets' red glare" came from. Unlike some men who tried to swallow her, this kiss had been tender. It made her toes curled. Her pulse pounded in her ears, though he'd said goodnight moments before.

She sprang up the stairs to her bedroom, changing into a long purple gown. Her cell phone went off as she sat on the edge of the bed. Looking at the caller ID, she broke into a smile.

"Hello." She attempted to hide her euphoria.

"Goodnight Lydia," Matthew said on the other end, reigniting the glare of the rockets.

"Goodnight." She laughed as she hung up.

She stretched out on the bed, replaying the evening in her mind. Rolling over, she snatched the picture of Justin from her bed stand. "Thank you for loving me enough to allow me to move on." She gently kissed the framed photograph as the cell went off again.

She slid her finger across the phone and Sheryl yelled, "I want to hear about your date and give me all the details!"

MATTHEW COULDN'T FORGET the way Lydia felt in his arms the night before. There was a bounce in his step as if in a mound of marshmallows. If things kept going the way there were, there would be a smile permanently etched on his face. He believed he'd met a lady he could spend the rest of his life with. She was not only beautiful, but intelligent and very caring, if her tears for Justin and her kindness of Jimmy were any indication. This was a woman who would make him a wonderful wife.

He stopped dead in his tracks. Before he met Lydia, he imagined he'd be the perpetual bachelor. But she changed all that. He smiled at words somebody had once told him: tell God your plan, he could use the laugh.

Maybe this might be a good time to bring up his involvement in Charlie's death, before he fell any deeper. He sat for a moment, going over the words in his head of what he would say. No words existed that would make her understand. He knew it was a secret he would have to hold to himself forever. For now, he would allow nothing to ruin his glorious mood.

Matthew dialed the phone and waited for his sister, Brenda, to answer.

"How are you this fine day, sis?" He sang into the telephone.

"You're in an awfully pleasant mood," Brenda said. "What's up?"

"I'm returning your call."

"I called to see if you had any plans for dinner next week on Sunday. The kids have been bugging me to get you over." Since coming to Lincolnville, Matthew had spent several evenings at his sister's. He hadn't realized how much he missed by being absent from his family. He wondered how her kids would react if he had children of his own. Sarah would be a built-in babysitter. Sonny would play baseball with his son. A grin straggled over him.

"That depends—" He caught the hesitation on the other end. "—On whether I can bring a guest."

"I figure when you come, Riley will probably be with you also. Besides, he's like part of the family."

"These days I don't find Riley that attractive. His masculine build doesn't do it for me anymore." Matthew laughed outright. "I'd rather bring someone else."

"You mean a woman?"

"She's definitely a woman." Matthew's heart thumped quickly as he recalled Lydia standing in the soft glow of the porch's light, her hair shining and her expression apprehensive.

"Is she special or just another of your typical dates where you love-'em and leave-'em?" He could hear humor in Brenda's question.

"Oh, she's special. And I have no intention of leaving her." Matthew added. "I only hope she has the same intention."

"Matthew, that's wonderful," Brenda cried out. "You'd better bring her by. I can't wait to meet her."

Upon hanging up from his sister, Matthew dialed Lydia's number.

"Good afternoon." Her voice was as provocative as the night before.

"Would you like to do dinner at my sister's on Sunday after next?"

When she agreed, Matthew had to fight to deter himself from shouting out loud. He grabbed his cell again as it rang. Riley. Talk about killing a great moment. "Why do I have a feeling you're about to ruin a wonderful mood, my friend?"

"Sorry." Riley responded. "Jimmy Newman's body was discovered in the woods off Caramel. His parents are on their way over. I'm sure Melanie could use you being there."

"I'm guessing a drug overdose."

"Try a bullet to the chest." There was a pause. "And Matthew, there was a Christmas gift tag attached to his shirt. It was addressed to Lydia."

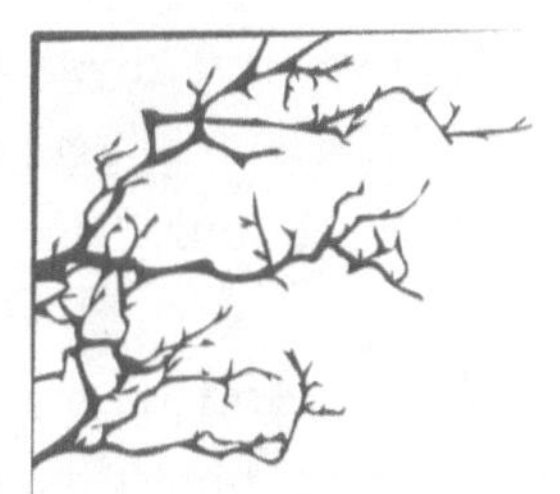

13

Memories of Justin's funeral flooded over Lydia as she stared at Jimmy's casket. She prayed he'd made his peace with God before he died. Matthew had officiated, his words compassionate and caring.

As Lydia stood with Sheryl to give her condolences to James and Melanie, she overheard funeral goers speculating about Jimmy's death.

"I heard he finally returned after being absent for several days," One woman said. "And he claimed it was Matthew who hurt Lydia. It made his mom mad, and she accused him of lying and falling back with his old habits. He stormed out, but not before stealing his mom's purse."

"How sad," another lady said. "The next evening, his body was found. Melanie must feel guilty over having the argument with her son."

The closer Lydia got to the front of the line, the more it appeared Melanie and James have aged years. Tears clung to James' eyes. Melanie's mascara-streaked face had dark circles, which made her face appear pale.

"I'm so sorry about Jimmy." Lydia extended her hand to James. She couldn't believe she had just seen him a week ago.

"All you had to do was pretend." James' look bore into her. "I wasn't asking you to spend the rest of your life with him, merely pretend for a little while. Just long enough for him to get well. You'll pay for this. One day you'll pay." James dabbed a white handkerchief to his face as he stalked off.

A lump rose in Lydia's throat. Maybe she should have done more to help Jimmy. Could she have been a better friend? Lydia lowered her head.

"It's not your fault." Melanie patted her wet cheeks with a tissue. "He couldn't see how Jimmy changed after the drugs. He was no longer that nice, kind boy we all remembered. If he had, maybe we could have done things differently."

"God was the only one who could have saved him. And Jimmy would have had to be receptive to His help." Lydia tried to suppress the guilt James raised in her. "I wish he had."

Melanie took Lydia's hand in hers. "You were a friend to him, and I know you cared. He knew that, too. And if you had given up your life for him, neither of you would have been happy. There really wasn't anything else you could have done."

Her words gave some modicum of comfort to Lydia. She prayed Melanie and James got through this ordeal.

Lydia dropped Sheryl off before driving home from the cemetery. As she cleaned some dishes from earlier, Matthew's motorcycle sounded.

"I thought you could use some company," he said, standing on the front porch. "Besides, I wanted to spend some time alone with you before you met my family. You'll probably hide yourself away from me after that."

"I can't imagine they're that bad. I'm sure I'll like them fine." Lydia hesitated. "I only hope they like me." Trepidation crept into her voice.

"Oh, they will. My dad fell for you the first day, and my sister's already making wedding plans."

The words rendered her speechless. Marriage. She hadn't even thought that far in advance. It felt as if a bolt of lightning surged through her. She imagined herself wide-eyed and her hair standing on end as smoke came out both of ears.

"She thinks you might be special since I'm willing to bring you over," Matthew said with an aloof hesitation. "It was a figure of speech."

"Oh, I see. And am I?"

"What?"

"Special?"

A blush ran over Matthew's cheeks as he avoided the question before saying, "I'll give you a chance to change while I pick up some fried chicken? I'll take you out for a picnic. It might help you get through the day."

"I'll be ready in a few minutes"

She tarried at the mirror to check her hair and her jeans and t-shirt. A wedding. This was the first time the thought had crossed her mind. Why did the mention of it shock her through to her toes? Because one day, she wouldn't mind becoming Mrs. Matthew Winters.

MATTHEW COULD'VE KICKED himself as he walked back to his bike, recalling how Lydia paled at the mere mention of a wedding. Why would she even be considering marriage? Much less to him, a man she barely knew. Matthew stopped abruptly. Why was he dwelling on it? All at once, his insides jumbled like a kid who rode a fast-spinning merry-go-round. Why was the idea of marrying Lydia even in his mind? They'd only known each other for a short time. The concept intrigued him.

After getting the chicken, he returned to find Lydia waiting on the front porch. She climbed on the bike behind him. With Lydia's arms encircling his waist, he drove to a rest area ten miles outside of Lincolnville. He couldn't wipe the smile off as he led her to a covered picnic area that lay behind a brick building. The wind caused the American flag on the roof to clap every few moments. The sun hung over them as they sat at a table near the woods.

"What are you smiling about?" Lydia raised her eyebrows. "You've got the look of the proverbial cat that ate the canary."

"I enjoy being with you, that's all." He was stunned at his good mood, considering the way the day began. He could only attribute it to the lovely woman walking beside him.

"You're full of baloney." Lydia slid onto a bench, with Matthew following. "This is a good idea, going to a rest area for a picnic," she said, placing a piece of fried chicken and a spoonful of potato salad on a paper plate.

"It's the perfect place. You have your covered tables, facilities close by, and some modicum of privacy." Matthew glanced at an older couple who sat a few tables behind them.

"Are you trying to get me alone, Matthew Winters?"

"Oh, yeah." He laughed.

"I wouldn't be surprised if Sheryl didn't have us followed, so she could let everyone know." Lydia glanced around as if looking for her. "She likes to be the first with the news."

"What did you do? Call her when I went for the food?"

"No. But I'm guessing one of my neighbors did." She grinned; her head tilted to the side.

"What's the deal with her and Riley?" Matthew had seen the sideways glances between the two and the teasing, but with Riley being so serious, he could actually mean the things he said.

"He cares for her, like a friend's pesky sister. She says all the time how attractive he is, but she's aware he has no interest in her. She's not really his type, anyway."

"What is his type?"

"He's kind of hard to figure, being so serious like he is." Lydia pulled back and looked at Matthew. "Why do you ask? Are you looking to fix him up?"

"I can't imagine everyone not being as in like as I am right now."

"In like. That's good."

"That's what it is." Matthew placed an arm around her shoulder. "So, what about Riley?"

"I don't know. I can't remember a time I've ever really seen him laugh or smile, and I mean, deep inside. He had planned to marry that woman who died in the robbery. They had a wedding date set and everything when she got killed."

"That had to have been a punch in the gut when he lost her." Matthew imagined if something happened to Lydia, he too might cease wanting to feel again.

He pushed her hair behind her ear. His fingers quivered as they mixed with brown tresses. He leaned in, breathing in the smell of gardenia. He really could spend the rest of his life feeling this way. Stroking the side of her neck, he felt her tremble.

Seconds before their lips met, a gunshot pierced the quietness of the afternoon.

"Are you hit?" Matthew pulled her to the ground.

"No."

A cry came from one of the pair seated behind them. The man slumped over and gripped his chest.

"He's been shot." Lydia gasped as she crawled toward the older couple, now on the ground. Blood seeped through the elder man's shirt. He groaned when his wife tried to pull his shirt away from his wound.

"Everyone stay down!" Matthew ordered, while dialing 911. He scanned the area for any sign of the gunman.

He prayed with the couple while they waited for the emergency crews to arrive. Upon arrival, EMTs placed the older man in an ambulance and his wife followed. The bullet had gone through his right shoulder.

The officers took Lydia and Matthew to a nearby station and placed them across the room from each other while they gave their statements. Matthew's eyes fixated on Lydia the whole time. His anxiety rose with each passing moment.

"Someone's been stalking Ms. Frederickson." Matthew spoke to the officer who took his statement. "Making phone calls, leaving pictures of her, things along that line. It's possible he's the person responsible."

"We'll look into it, but it's not unusual to have hunters follow game down this way," the officer said as a dog bayed in the distance. "It was probably some guy who lost his bearings and didn't realize he was shooting toward a rest area."

However, in Matthew's gut, something gnawed. He knew the caller had just sent a very dangerous message.

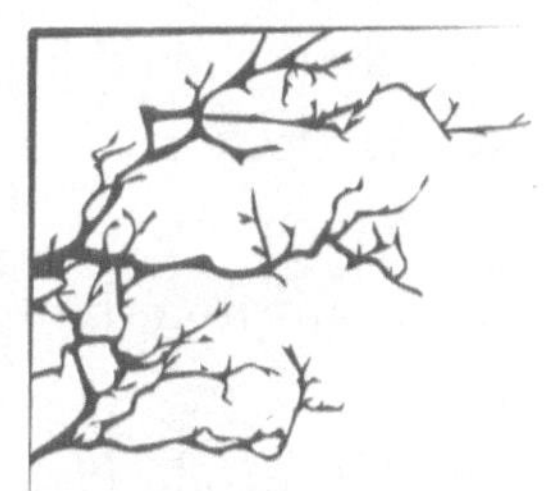

14

Why was she so nervous about meeting Matthew's family? Whenever he spoke of his sister, the tone told her of their closeness. Lydia hoped the evening went smoothly. She was worried they might have enough influence to convince him to not see her again if things didn't go well.

She wore a pair of jeans and a yellow pullover cashmere sweater with her leather jacket to keep the cool October night air out. Her hair sat in a ponytail. After all, a helmet would mess up any style she tried. Silver balls for earrings, a silver chain surrounded her wrist, and a cross necklace decorated as accessories. She glanced in the mirror and pushed back loose strands of hair.

She glanced at the ringing telephone. Caller I.D. said it was Sheryl. They chitchatted while Lydia brushed some blush across her cheeks.

"Meeting the family. That's a big deal, isn't it?" Sheryl said over the telephone.

Lydia's heart pounded in her chest. Please let everything go well.

"I'm not sure how big a deal it is." Lydia's response may have implied nonchalance, but her nerves said anything but.

There had been no movement from her stalker in the last couple of days, including phone calls. If the bullet at the rest area had been closer to her, she would have deemed it a warning, but for now, she had to conclude it had been a stray bullet as the police claimed. She hoped the maniac had given up his cruel pranks.

"So, how are you getting there?" Sheryl said. "Not on that bike, I hope."

125

"It's not that far. Besides, it's a fabulous day and there should be only a slight breeze in the evening." Glancing at the clock on her nightstand, Lydia realized Matthew would be there any moment.

"Have you gotten a call from Warren? I haven't heard from him since he left." A hint of worry carried in Sheryl's voice.

Even though it'd been about a week, Lydia missed her friend. "He's probably busy with his new job and making friends."

"I hope he calls. I want to make sure everything's going well."

"He probably forgot to charge his cell with all the excitement." Lydia glanced one last time in the mirror. "You sound like a mother whose kid went off to college."

"I'm worried about him out there all alone."

"I wish he had let us go with him, so we could have found him a place to live," Lydia said. "Even if Matthew knows this friend he's staying with, he's a stranger to Warren."

"Now who's sounding like a college kid's mom?" Sheryl laughed. "Be careful out there on that bike."

"You worry too much. Besides, it's fun. Things have been too serious lately."

"But exactly how safe is a motorbike?"

"This from the girl who started snowboarding at thirteen to capture the attention of a boy." Lydia chuckled. "There's little doubt in my mind, you'll end up with a bike of your own and be out there cruising with us on the weekends."

"Do me a favor Lydia, make sure Matthew keeps it slow. I'd hate to see you hurt."

"I will." Lydia couldn't tell whether Sheryl referred to the bike ride or her emotional state. As she contemplated the answer, a loud roar sounded in front of her house.

THE TEMPERATURES HAD been sitting in the upper fifties for days, making the ride wonderful. Lydia felt free and invigorated as they pulled up to the green and white house. The front curtain swung into place when she climbed off the bike.

"Are you sure you're ready for this? They can be a bit much." Matthew attached the helmets to the bike. "We can always hop on and ride off into the sunset."

"I believe that would be rude. With all the gossip we've had to endure since you've gotten to town, this should be a walk in the park." Matthew appeared more nervous than she did. "Besides, they already know we're here," Lydia whispered, pointing toward the window, the drapes still swaying.

"Let's go. But remember, when all's said and done, I did warn you." He led her to the front door of the house.

Brenda's inviting welcome caused any nervousness Lydia had to disappear. Her husband Richard stooped over a grill on the side patio. George Winters, enormous smile told of his happiness at meeting her again. Sonny, Brenda's fourteen-year-old, gave her hand a firm shake, while Sarah, the preteen, stood against the far wall and only nodded when introduced.

"I'm so glad you could make it," Mr. Winters said, giving her hand a gentle squeeze.

"Me, too. How are you?"

"Excellent, now that I have a pretty girl beside me." He winked.

Brenda led them into a tan colored den where a beige sofa held faded burgundy pillows on each arm. A matching recliner sat beside a wicker, high-back chair with a flowered cushion. Several pictures of the kids, all at different stages of their life, hung around the area in matching white frames.

"I'm sorry; it's a bit crowded in here." Brenda had awkwardness to her tone. "We've contemplated buying new furniture but haven't decided exactly how to redecorate it."

"I like how you have it." Lydia caressed the softness of the pillow beside her. "It feels warm and inviting, a home with kids."

"Matthew tells me you don't have any children." Brenda's shoulders eased.

"No. At least, not yet."

They sat around discussing the kids, her job, Matthew's job, the usual getting-to-know-you-chat to fill the time. Finally, a lull fell over the conversation.

"Here, let me show you the landscape." Mr. Winters stood, requesting her arm to guide her. "It'll give us a chance to talk about my son's wild side, so you'll have time to make your break before it's too late."

"You don't need to fill her in on any of that," Matthew hollered as Mr. Winters led Lydia to the wood deck out back.

Azalea bushes that lined the white fence surrounding the property no longer held their blooms. Leaves from magnolia trees cascaded over from the neighboring yard. They drooped like kids hanging over the sides trying to enter. In the spring, with big white blooms draped within the azaleas, Lydia imagined the yard held a magnificent view.

"So, what's this about Matthew's wild side? I'd better get as much information before I fall in any deeper than I already am." Lydia bumped Mr. Winters lightly with her shoulder.

"Oh, he's always been a pretty good boy. A bit of a rebel at times." He stared off as he spoke. "Purchasing that bike. It worries Brenda, him driving it all over. Not that he's not an apt driver. She just worries."

"And you?"

"And me." A faraway look slid over Mr. Winters. "He fell away from God for a while. Never got into really bad trouble. A few women he shouldn't have been with, but that's about it. I'm glad he's back."

"I am, too," Lydia said. The smell of barbeque from the front drifted over her. She prayed her stomach didn't growl.

Mr. Winters told her bits and piece about Matthew's childhood and his becoming a minister. Pride carried in his voice with each word.

"He hasn't scared you too bad, has he?" Brenda walked through the back door. "Dad, it's a bit chilly out. Maybe you'd better come in."

Mr. Winters tilted his head toward Lydia. "That's her way of telling me she wants to talk to you alone. Just remember, her bark's worse than her bite."

"Dad!" Brenda then said, "My bite's pretty bad." She waited until her dad was inside before speaking. "I hope he didn't bore you." Brenda stood in the same place her father had been seconds earlier. "He can sometimes go on at great length with his stories."

"I enjoyed it. He was giving me some history on Matthew." Lydia angled slightly toward Brenda. "He's a nice man."

"My dad or Matthew?" Brenda gave a small grin.

"Both." Lydia responded with a chuckle.

"You're the first woman Matthew's brought home for the family to meet." Wisps of Brenda's blonde hair blew in the gentle breeze.

"He told me. He said you all were quite excited."

"A bit. I'd like for him to settle down. Somewhere close, preferably?"

"Don't worry. I'm a Georgia girl, born and raised. I'm not planning on leaving." How presumptive, making it sound as if they'd be spending their lives together. If his sister told Matthew about their conversation, would it be enough to scare him off?

Brenda nudged Lydia with her hand as they looked out over the yard. Gradually a smile came over both women, giving Lydia ease. She had nothing to worry about.

The clicking of cowboy boots sounded in the kitchen, leading to the patio. The smell of spice infiltrated Lydia's mind and emotions.

"Let me guess, she's giving away all my childhood secrets?" Matthew placed his hand on Lydia's back.

"I wouldn't think to do that. At least not on the first meeting." Brenda grinned at her brother. "That's always saved for after you're married. Then she'd be stuck and couldn't run off."

"That bad, huh?" Lydia missed that type of teasing. She recalled how she and Charlie used to go after each other when they were young before he got into drugs. If Charlie had lived and gotten straight, would they have become close again? A lump rose in her throat.

"I'm not saying another word." Brenda put her hands up in a surrender motion. "Excuse me while I look into what kind of mess my husband's making in my kitchen."

"What can I do to help?" Lydia offered, taking her focus off her brother's death. "I'm pretty capable in a kitchen."

"You're a guest. You two stay out here and enjoy the peace for a moment." She gave Matthew a wink before leaving.

"Pretty and you can cook, too. I like that in a woman" Matthew smiled. "How are you holding up?"

His breath tickled her ear as she rested against his shoulder. "Your family is wonderful. Your niece doesn't seem to care for me, though. She continually glares."

"According to Richard, she's afraid you're going to break my heart, and I'll move, and she'll never see me again."

"That's so sweet." With Matthew's arms around her, Lydia shivered. How could she have such intense feelings for someone she hardly knew?

THE SCENT COMING FROM Lydia's hair made Matthew's knees knock. The sun drifted slowly below the magnolias as they stood together. Matthew couldn't decide which he believed more beautiful, the yellow and orange display in the sky or the woman standing next to him with her head against his shoulder.

When she looked up at him, he bent his head, and their lips met. His lips stroked hers, first lightly, then closer and deeper, sending him soaring.

"Dinner's ready!" Sonny yelled from inside the kitchen. His brown hair blew in the breeze when he stepped out onto the deck. "That is, if you can tear yourselves from each other long enough to eat."

"I guess we'd better go in," Lydia said. A blush ran over her nose.

The velvety tone caused Matthew's throat to constrict. He could barely speak as he led her inside.

All during dinner, he kept looking in her direction. She had his insides all churned up. When she returned his glance, he turned to liquid all over.

"Uncle Matthew, are you in there?" Sonny snapped his fingers in front of Matthew's nose.

"I'm sorry. My mind wandered." Matthew wiped his mouth with his napkin as he adjusted in his chair, doing his best to regain his composure.

"It doesn't take much to figure out where it wandered to, or *who* it wandered to," Sonny said with a large grin.

Warmth rushed into Matthew when he caught sight of Lydia over the rim of his glass. Her cheeks had gone a shade of pink. She captured his heart all over again.

"I asked if Riley would be coming over soon. He promised to work on my curve ball."

"I'll find out and let you know." At no other time did Matthew have such trouble focusing his attention than during this evening.

"Sarah, it's time to clear the dishes," Brenda said. "I believe it's your turn."

Sarah groaned.

"Do what your mother tells you." Richard replied.

"How about I help?" Lydia stood. "After all, you have more dishes than normal, so it wouldn't be fair to make you do it alone."

"Let me guess," Sarah murmured with a roll of her blue eyes. "You remember having to do it as a kid."

"Sarah!" Brenda shot her daughter a stern look.

"Not me. The maid did it." Lydia continued as if she hadn't detected the sarcasm in Sarah's tone. It told Matthew she would make a wonderful mother, especially once her children became teenagers.

"You have a maid?" Sarah stopped. Her mouth opened as she stared at Lydia. She brushed blonde strands from her face while holding an armload of dishes.

"My parents did," Lydia said. The others also had opened mouths. "My dad did very well in the stock market in the '80s. Also, they owned Liberty Lodge on the hill."

"Me and my friends go there snowboarding every winter." Sonny's volume went up an octave. His green eyes widened with amazement. "So, you know how to ski?"

"That's a prerequisite for being born into the family." Lydia carried a handful of plates into the kitchen followed by Sarah, who had yet to close her mouth. Sonny followed.

"I swear sometimes it's like pulling teeth getting her to do any measly amount of work anymore." Brenda sighed.

"I remember a teenage girl once who kept her clothes piled in a laundry basket instead of hanging them in the closet." Matthew teased his sister. "Once she wore the clothes, they would end up in a pile in the corner. I swear Mt. Everest looked small in comparison."

"It wasn't that bad." Brenda smacked at him with her napkin. "If I recall, you weren't exactly a neat nick yourself."

His father chuckled. "There for a while, I wasn't convinced there was a floor in his room."

"I had to keep it a mess. When mom finished cleaning the outer area, she was too tired to do under my bed where I kept a secret stash of girlie magazines." Matthew leaned toward Brenda. "Long before my Christian days."

"I would hope so," Brenda said. "I'd hate to imagine those magazines are still there."

"So, what do you think of Lydia?" Matthew sipped from his glass of iced tea. Their opinion meant more to him than he realized.

"She's nice, intelligent, and pretty." Mr. Winters offered.

"I agree. The best part, it's obvious how much you care for her." Brenda grabbed hold of her brother's hand from across the table. "I hope you don't blow it."

"Me, too." He gave Brenda a squeeze as Lydia returned, closely followed by Sarah who was giggling. Sonny entered a few seconds later with a piece of fried chicken he'd apparently retrieved from the refrigerator.

"I can't seem to fill that boy up," Brenda said.

Matthew watched as Lydia and Sarah finished clearing the table, both talking and laughing as if close friends.

"I believe Sarah's coming around," Matthew whispered when the preteen returned to the kitchen. "What happened?"

"Apparently, she's a big fan of theatre and we discussed maybe driving to Atlanta to catch a show," Lydia said. "That's if it's okay with her mother."

"You can take her anytime." A huge smile came over Brenda. "After the wedding."

"Brenda!" Matthew cast his sister a glare.

"That's also when I learn all the bad stuff about Matthew, isn't it?" Lydia threw him a wink that caused pleasure to flood into his chest.

They spent the rest of the evening laughing and talking about their families. Brenda even asked her about Justin. Matthew could tell Lydia appreciated it. It neared eleven when they headed back to Lincolnville. The temperature had dropped considerably, so he insisted she wear his jacket over her own. Once her arms encircled him, his body heat would rise.

"I had a wonderful evening. Your family's terrific." Lydia led him up the steps to her front door, his hand on her back. He waited with her while she unlocked the door and turned on the light inside.

"They liked you too." Matthew lifted her chin, staring into her eyes. His desire to dance in them grew. Their lips touched, not just a whisper of a kiss. They melded together. He had to remind his heart to beat once they finished. He had never cared for anyone with every ounce of his spirit. Earlier, as he held her on the patio, he realized he'd fallen in love. The awareness practically knocked him over.

He walked down the porch and stood beside his bike. Lights glowed from within the house. Even when he tried to force it, the smile wouldn't leave. He looked at the clear night sky. "As you said, Sis, and with God's blessings, I hope I don't blow it." Lydia had him feeling positively giddy. It wouldn't surprise him at all if he giggled out loud. For the first time in his life, he was in love, and he planned to savor it. He wondered if the neighbors would notice if he jumped in the air.

As he slid the helmet over his head, he heard Lydia scream.

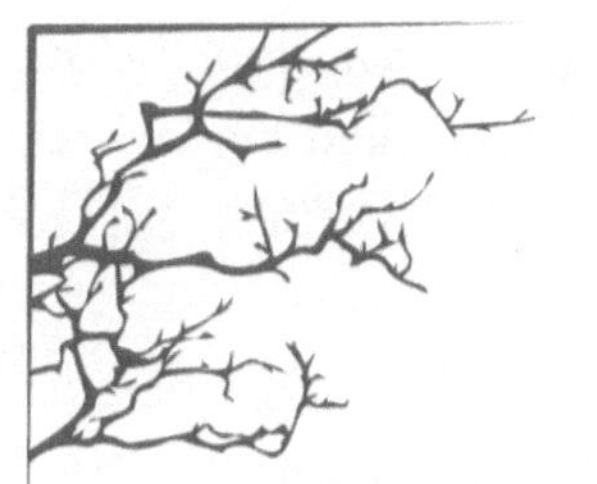

15

Matthew broke through the front door on his third try. The piercing scream shook him to the core. As he ran through the house, he called out Lydia's name. He found her slunk down against the wall outside the upstairs bedroom, trembling.

"Lydia." He lowered to one knee beside her.

She sat motionless, ghostly white, staring straight ahead. A dark color caught his attention. He walked into the bedroom. Someone had covered the bed and walls with what appeared to be red paint. Stuffing from a mattress covered the room. A purple silk nightgown lay in shreds. The words YOU ARE MINE scrawled in red above the bed. He had enough experience to recognize the color came from blood. Matthew punched in the number from memory.

"Riley. I'm at Lydia's. Get over here. Now!" Anger crawled inside. He didn't wait for a response before cutting the call off.

He paused, a reflection from the overhead light catching his attention. Near the foot of the bed lay a small badge pendant with raised initials that read APD. He recognized it as being worn by members of the Atlanta Police Department.

Lydia's whimper pulled him back to the hallway. She held her knees against her chest, rocking back and forth, her eyes wide with fear. He knelt to raise her from the ground, but she slapped at him as he lifted her. Her fists thrashed as she screamed, trying to free herself from his grip.

"It's okay. You're safe. No one's going to hurt you." He struggled to pull her to him as her arms flailed. Her fists pounded his chin and chest. Finally, she stopped, falling against him, sobbing.

135

Picking her up, he carried her to the couch on the floor below. She clung tightly to him, crying into his neck. He pulled her tighter. Whoever did this invaded the very place she should have been able to find rest and comfort.

"You're safe. He's not here anymore." He tugged a nearby blanket from the back of the sofa and placed it over her. "I've got you, it's okay." Sirens finally announced the sheriff. "Riley's here."

She froze in place, there in his arms, her body quivering. It killed him forcing her arms away from his neck. When he rose, she grabbed a pillow, clinging as if it a life vest, and she floated in the middle of a desolate ocean.

Riley entered first, followed by two other officers.

"Upstairs." Matthew nodded toward the staircase. Riley stopped short when he saw Lydia. He took a quick glance at Matthew before ascending to the second floor. Riley's look of concern made it hard for Matthew to believe he was the person responsible. However, the pendant moved him to the top of the suspect list in Matthew's mind. But deep inside, he knew Riley would never do this.

Matthew returned to the sofa and wrapped his arm around Lydia. He held her tight, hoping the trembling would subside. Sounds of bewilderment drifted from the bedroom upstairs. Within seconds, footsteps descended.

"Lydia. Are you okay?" Riley knelt beside the couch, pushing her hair to the side.

Her grip tightened on Matthew's arm at Riley's touch. Her body went from lightly trembling to outright shaking.

"It's all right. You're safe now." Mathew kept his tone quiet while holding her. As much as he wanted to rant about who did this, Matthew knew he had to remain calm, for Lydia's sake.

Riley brushed a hand over his mouth, his jaw locked into place, and his lips pierced tight. "Forensic people should be arriving soon. Until then, we need to get her out of here." He pulled out his cell phone. "Sheryl, sorry to wake you."

Matthew listened as Riley told Sheryl what happened.

Riley again knelt beside Lydia. "Sheryl's coming over. She's taking you to her house to stay for a while." He looked at Matthew. "I'm posting a man outside Sheryl's as an added precaution. You'll have to stay and let us know what happened. She's not in any shape to talk at the moment."

If Riley was the person responsible, he should receive an Academy Award for his performance. He showed nothing but distress for Lydia. There had to be another explanation for that pendant being upstairs.

Matthew's tone came out low and lethal as he spoke, "You best get the guy who's doing this, because God help him if I discover who he is first."

MATTHEW LEANED AGAINST a squad car as he waited for the forensic unit from Catoosa County in Ringgold, Georgia to finish. Sheryl had left with Lydia a couple of hours ago. She was still trembling as Sheryl drove her away.

His anger seethed as he recalled the expression held by Lydia. It started as a wonderful day. A day with him realizing he was in love. How could it have ended this way? The more he thought about it, the more he wanted to hit something, or someone.

"We're about done here." Riley watched as the technicians left the scene. "Lydia will have to go through to let us know if anything's missing."

"Did you come up with any evidence of who did this?" Matthew had yet to unclench his fists.

"I can't discuss an ongoing case."

"I asked if you came up with any indication of who did this." Matthew repeated his question slowly, with more force.

Riley ran his fingers atop the stubble on his chin. "I can tell you this much. There appears to be no forced entry; at least that we could see with the front door torn apart. But there are too many snoopy neighbors to break in that way." He scanned the crowd gathered outside the police crime tape. "Whoever did this must have a key. We won't know if anything's stolen until Lydia checks things out."

"And?"

"I'm not overly confident what we discovered will amount to much." Riley looked at the house, away from the people staring and whispering. "This guy seems to know what he's doing."

"How about that pendant on the bedroom floor?" Matthew grabbed Riley by the collar of his shirt and shoved him into the police car. His voice quieted as he spewed venom from behind closed teeth. "Did your forensic team find it or had it disappeared by the time they got here?"

"Hey, calm yourself." Riley held up his hands. "It was there," he whispered. "But I'm telling you, it was planted. I haven't been in that room since Justin was sick."

Matthew stared at his friend before slowly releasing his jacket. "I'm sorry. I can't get the image of her sitting on that floor, staring wide-eyed in fear. You didn't have her fists punching at you as she neared hysterics."

"Get control of yourself. The last thing Lydia needs is for you to lose your temper and go around beating on people." Riley adjusted his clothes back into place.

Matthew scratched his thumb against his forehead. "It's how I've handled things in the past." He shoved his fingers through his hair before settling his hands on his hips. He then noticed astonished expressions on the people standing about.

"It wouldn't be decent for a Christian man to strike a sheriff. Especially if that Christian happened to also be a preacher." Riley glanced in the crowd's direction. "I guess God's still working with you in that area."

"I suppose." Matthew muttered, before walking to his bike. He craved solace. There was only one place he would achieve peace. "I'll be at the church."

MATTHEW WALKED INTO the chapel, turning on the light over the stage. It cascaded over the pulpit. His pulpit. The place where he stood, indicating he was a righteous man. Righteous didn't come near to how he'd describe himself at that moment. He had lost his temper and came close to hitting someone. Losing control brought about an ache to his gut.

He'd been working to get his courage up to tell Lydia about his past. Sleep hadn't been forthcoming. There would be no way he could tell her now. He knew he would find no solace in rest again tonight.

A humbling feeling crawled over him, a man who prided himself on being able to solve problems for others. He recalled how in Nashville he'd worked with former abusers, showing them how to turn to God instead of their fists to deal with any issues that arose. The hypocrisy hardly escaped him.

He stared at the cross hanging in the front. With the lights on over the stage, it appeared to have a halo. Tears fell as he walked forward, crumbling to his knees.

"Please God, forgive me," he pleaded. "Please forgive me for losing my temper tonight. And please forgive me for those times I've lost it in the past, expecting others to tolerate it." He openly sobbed in the empty sanctuary. "Please God, help me keep control of my emotions in the future and to realize there are external things I can't control. But I can control the internal feelings. And please help me help Lydia by giving her inner strength and comfort now, not brute force. Please Lord; let her feel your loving arms holding her. And Lord, please help me find the right words and time to tell her the secret I've kept hidden. At that time, help her to forgive me."

The thought of losing Lydia, whether to a killer or his own actions, ate at him. And he knew losing his temper in front of a crowd had been the price he paid. He raised himself onto a seat and stared up at that wonderful cross.

Lydia's fear still burned him to his core. Worry sunk deep inside as he recalled grabbing Riley. He pondered over what he would have done if he had caught Lydia's terrorist in the house. How far would he have gone? Would he have forgotten his faith to feel his hands around the man's throat?

LYDIA RECALLED COMING up the stairs to see her bedroom destroyed. A loud scream emanated from her throat. Someone grabbed at her. It took seconds fighting them off before she realized it was Matthew. Thank you, God, for the safety of his strong arms.

She wasn't sure how she got to Sheryl's. She was unsure who had removed her shoes, she or Sheryl. Now she curled under a blanket. Shrouded in a fog, Lydia finally realized she was in her friend's guest bedroom.

Blackness enveloped her while she listened to sounds of the dark. Light from the hallway cast a shadow over a figure off to her right. Sheryl lay curled on a settee under the window.

Lydia shuddered. Her stalker had been in her house, in her bedroom. He had destroyed everything. She ran over all the people she knew, but no person came to mind who hated her so much they would cut and slash at her with such madness. What would have happened if he'd been there when she entered? And if Matthew had come in for coffee? She gripped the blanket into her fists, hoping to release the damp fingers of terror that choked her. Beads of sweat covered her forehead. She prayed for comfort and prayed they discovered who was doing this. The last thing she wanted was to spend the rest of her life looking over her shoulder.

Everyone had thoughts of death. Even she had, especially after Justin's illness. But almost coming face to face with the prospect caused a tremor in her body. The realization crept in that it wasn't about scaring her anymore.

He wanted to kill her.

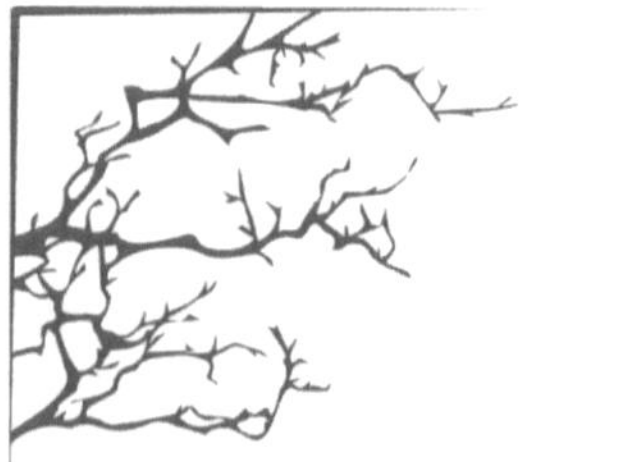

<h1 style="text-align:center">16</h1>

At a little past nine the next morning, Matthew sat in his car outside Sheryl's home. He waited, praying, attempting to find the correct words to comfort Lydia. Sleep had escaped him last night. Memories of Charlie Westerman's death haunted the long night. The blood in the bedroom reminded Matthew of the blood in the alleyway.

The deep green grass, along with the neatly trimmed hedges, gave him a sense of order. He sauntered up the stone walkway. Four large pillars ran along the front porch, and a beveled glass door, decorated with a lily, greeted him as he approached. He paused for a moment and prayed silently again for strength before knocking.

Sheryl answered and led him to the kitchen. "She'll be okay once she's over the initial shock. She actually slept pretty well." Sheryl passed him a mug of coffee after he sat at the dining room table. "I stayed with her in case she needed me. I wish Warren hadn't left yet. He always had a way of making her feel better, no matter the circumstances."

"You're a good friend." From the dark circles, it was clear Sheryl hadn't had much rest either.

The beige dining area had an oriental flare he hadn't noticed when he visited before. White serving bowls glared from the glass cabinets and offered a stark contrast to the dark wood furniture. A large white pendant light hung over the table, giving off a soft glow. A painting of a Chinese woman holding a fan hung on the wall. The signature at the bottom read S. Coufield. Lydia was right, Sheryl was very talented.

"I wish we knew who was doing this." Sheryl rose to answer the ringing doorbell. "Have they found out anything?" She led Riley in.

142

Matthew felt a large lump as he rose to eat his actions from the night before. He'd wanted to hurt somebody for hurting Lydia, and he chose his friend, even though he knew deep down Riley couldn't be responsible.

"How's she doing?" Riley asked, as Sheryl went to get him some coffee.

"She's still sleeping. She apparently slept pretty good once she arrived."

Riley nodded.

He wore a pair of dark blue jeans and a plain black t-shirt. Quite a contrast to his tan uniform. Riley retreated with Matthew to the living-room.

"And you, how are you doing?" Riley leaned against the fireplace to the left of a brown sofa. Two additional paintings caught Matthew's eye. One held a waterfall, the other a village. Both, again, signed S. Coufield.

"I'm a bit calmer," Matthew said through steam from the mug of coffee. "Listen, about last night. I want to apologize. I had no reason to attack you, verbally or otherwise."

"It's okay. Besides, if it had been me and a woman I cared for, I would have landed the blow." Riley gave a slight turn of his head. "But then, I'm not a preacher."

When Sheryl joined them, Lydia followed behind. Matthew was relieved to see the color had returned to her face. She allowed him to pull her into a hug, her cheek resting on his chest. Even if he had no words of comfort, he could hold her and let her know he cared.

She tried to force a smile. "I'm sorry I'm such a mess," she said.

"I think you look wonderful." He brushed her hair from her cheek. "We'll figure out who's doing this. Don't you worry."

She turned around and leaned back against the crook of his shoulder. His deep-rooted anger had dissipated. All Matthew wanted to do was protect her from this maniac who'd entered her life. There was no way he was bringing up her brother's shooting now. It would only cause her more pain.

"The telephone calls and the picture were bad enough, but now he's been in my house." Lydia lifted herself as she spoke to Riley. "Do they have any new information?"

"They have a suspect, but that's all."

"Who? Who did this?" Sheryl had fire in her eyes. "You give me five minutes alone with him, and I'll force a confession."

"I'm afraid I can't do that." Riley drew his eyes to the floor. "Besides, I know for a fact he didn't do it."

"How can you be so positive?" Sheryl folded her arms across her chest. "Let me guess, it's a crony at the station. It's like the big city. All you cops stick together and protect each other."

"It's not that," Riley answered. He ran a hand down his face. His eyes were bloodshot and tired. Lack of sleep seemed to be a common denominator among the four.

"Who do they suspect it is?" Lydia's voice sounded desperate. "Please tell me. I need to know."

Riley inhaled deeply and shot Matthew an anxious look. "They think it's me."

THE POLICE DISCOVERED a badge-shaped pendant at the foot of her bed. One like Riley owned. Lydia's mind ran over plausible scenarios. She could only think of two. Either he had to be the person terrorizing her or someone placed it there to implicate him.

"It's not only the pin." Anxiety rode over Riley's features as he took a deep breath.

A chill raced through Lydia at what could be next.

"What more could there be?" Sheryl's tone held the trepidation Lydia felt.

"The bullet used to kill Jimmy Newman came from a gun I kept at my house." He stared into the waterfall painting over the fireplace. "I'm being set up real well. I've been put on leave of absence from the department. The Sheriff in Ringgold and his people have taken over the investigation." He turned to Lydia. "We kept everything quiet, hoping someone would mention some evidence and give themselves away. I guess most of the information will come out now." His voice went low when he said, "A note was found on Jimmy's body. It was a Christmas gift tag to you."

Lydia felt a punch in the midsection. This maniac shot Jimmy because of her. White dots appeared before her as everything spun.

"Lydia." Sheryl rushed to her side.

"I'm feeling a bit claustrophobic." She staggered. The stress of the previous evening crashed over her. Her hands trembled, and her knees folded beneath her as she caved against Matthew.

He led her outside to a white swing on the front porch. The plush cushion welcomed her as she leaned back. Fresh air relaxed her, and the haziness dissipated. She choked in a deep breath. Once composed, she ran over everything in her mind.

"Lydia, I am not doing this to you. I would never hurt you," Riley pleaded. "I didn't kill Jimmy, and I didn't break into your house. You have to believe me."

She swallowed hard and brushed a hand through her hair. "When we found out about Justin's illness, I was devastated. I saw everything I'd dreamed for us dying, too. He said no matter what happened, three things I could always be sure of. First and foremost, trust my faith in God; second, never doubt his love for me."

"And the third?" Matthew placed his arm on the back of the swing.

"You can always trust Riley Owens."

"That much is true. I know that from experience," Matthew said.

"I can't imagine if he trusted you that much, you would betray him by terrifying me." Lydia reached out and placed Riley's hand in hers. "I know you aren't doing this to me." She choked back any tears. "And I know you weren't the person who killed Jimmy."

Riley gave her hand a squeeze. "Thank you. That means a lot to me." Tears rose in Riley's eyes.

"Has it occurred to you that maybe you're the intended target?" Matthew looked at the three.

"What do you mean?" Riley stared down at Matthew.

"Maybe it's not really Lydia who this guy's after. He starts by making telephone calls on the anniversary of *your* close friend's death. Most people are aware you would probably check on her. He uses office supplies from *your* office, and he puts a photograph at the gravesite of *your* friend, fully aware you would be there to see it."

Long nails ran up Lydia's spine. The more Matthew discussed the matter, the more her anxiety level rose.

"Then he destroys her house to plant evidence implicating you." Matthew continued. "It could be it's you he's been after all along."

"They could have gotten into my house and taken the gun while I was working. It's not exactly Fort Knox." Riley added. "It's probably when they got the pendant. I kept it on my dresser."

"If so, it's someone who's familiar with your and Lydia's relationship." Matthew rose.

"So, what you're saying is Riley is the person he's after." Lydia gave Matthew a worried look. "I'm just a means to an end."

"A way to get even with Riley for something he'd done, whether it be real or imagined," Matthew replied.

Sheryl glanced up and down the street. "He could be watching us. If so, it won't take long before he realizes his plan didn't work. He probably hoped we'd turn against Riley, leave him out to blow in the wind by himself, so to speak."

Lydia's fear had morphed into anger as she rose. "I'm not about to let this jerk use me like that. I'm tired of giving this guy all the power and feeling as if I'm a victim. Maybe I should start fighting back." She paced the porch. "I'm going to go to my house and clean it to show everyone I'm not his pawn."

"It's still considered a crime scene," Riley said. "They won't release it for a couple more days. The forensic guys are going over it again to make sure my people didn't miss anything."

"Once they're finished, I'll clean it up." Lydia gave a curt nod. "He'll see, I'm not afraid."

The weight that had been on her chest lifted. Lydia could actually breathe again. She saw concern in her friends' eyes as they stood around her. "Don't worry. I won't get carried away. I probably sound braver than I really feel." Lydia grinned.

Matthew took her hand in his. "Good. Because I wonder how far he'll go to take revenge on Riley."

LYDIA HAD STAYED WITH Sheryl for three days when the police said her house would be available by the weekend. She would be glad to get inside and see how much damage there was. She only hoped she didn't freak out upon seeing her bedroom. It was too bad Warren had already left. She could use all the support she could get. Not that he returned any of their calls. They'd only received a couple of texts with brief messages saying he was trying to focus on his work.

Was he so busy, he no longer had time for his old friends? Maybe she should be happy he's doing well in his new life.

She looked at paint samples between she and Sheryl while seated in the booth at the small sandwich shop in Chattanooga. "I feel good about redoing the house once we're finished upstairs. Some of your ideas will work nice to open it up and make it feel more alive. That should make Riley happy."

"And the new man coming over," Sheryl said.

"I'm not sure we should continue to see each other until they catch this guy. What if he's not really after Riley, but I'm the target?" Lydia sucked in a breath. "I couldn't handle it again if I lost anyone else I cared for that deeply."

"What do you mean by that deeply?" A coy smile crossed Sheryl's face. "Come on. Say it out loud."

Lydia's face warmed at the thought of Matthew's arms around her. Her feelings for him had deepened the last couple of weeks. She was surprised by how much she cared for him, though they had only known each other a short time.

"I thought that was your car parked outside."

Lydia startled at James Newman, III standing over them. She got the uneasy feeling of being watched. She swallowed hard and worked to regain her composure. "James, how are you and Melanie doing?"

"We're adjusting." He paused. "I spoke with Riley yesterday. I understand his gun was used to kill my son."

"He told us." Sheryl wiped the condensation from her glass of tea.

"I also discovered he'd been removed from office until you interfered." James glared down at Lydia. "You used the Pendleton influence to get him reinstated."

"We all know he's not guilty. He's obviously being set up." She tried to hold her voice down so other patrons couldn't hear. "Besides, I didn't use any influence. Riley was able to account for his whereabouts between the time I left home and the time I returned. There's no way he could have done it."

"All I know is you're assisting the person who possibly killed my son. You can't imagine what this is doing to Melanie."

"She'll be fine once the actual killer is discovered. Maybe if I call and talk with her," Lydia offered.

"You will do no such thing." James slammed his hand on the table. "You should mind your own business. If you think those phone calls are bad, you have no idea the type of damage I can do." He rose and folded his arms across his chest. "You really didn't turn out to be the type of woman I thought you were."

"I'm sorry I disappointed you, James." Lydia fought to keep from rolling her eyes. His pious attitude irritated her.

"You help a killer get off, and you date the man who shot your brother. I wonder what your parents would say if they ever found out."

Lydia's heart leapt into her throat. *The man who shot my brother.* "What are you talking about?"

"Don't tell me your preacher lover didn't tell you he's the one who shot Charlie in Miami."

"I don't believe you." Lydia wanted to knock the smug look from James' face, but she was too stunned to move. She looked at Sheryl, whose eyes had widened, and mouth hung open.

James leaned on the table with one hand. "Contact the Miami-Dade Police Department. They'll tell you. I guess that new boyfriend of yours isn't as straightforward as you think. I'm sure once everyone in the congregation finds out, they'll be more than happy to deal with Matthew appropriately." James turned and strutted out.

Lydia couldn't speak. She couldn't catch her breath. Not once since they met did Matthew mention knowing Charlie. Lydia never would have dated him, much less fallen in — The thought stood at the forefront of her mind. How could she care for someone who killed her brother? Nausea rose.

"Lydia. Lydia." Sheryl touched Lydia's hand, bringing her attention from her thoughts. "It's not true. You know Matthew. He'd never kill anyone."

"He used to be with the DEA. It was part of his job. Besides, how do we know what he was like before he came to God?" Tears filled her eyes.

"James isn't happy unless everyone's as miserable as he is." Sheryl grabbed Lydia's hand. "I'm sure Matthew had nothing to do with Charlie's death."

"There's only one way to find out, isn't there?" Lydia shoved her chair out and threw a twenty on the table. If Matthew was the person who killed her brother, she could never forgive him.

MATTHEW PULLED THE book from the upper tier of the bookcase. He nearly toppled off the ladder when he heard his door open, and someone stormed in. When he turned around, Lydia was there. Sheryl stood behind her, pale, and for the first time since he'd met her, quiet. His excitement quickly turned to anxiety as his stomach knotted at the look on Lydia's face. She clenched her jaw, and tears stood in her eyes.

"What's wrong?" Matthew said. "Did something else happen?"

"Did you shoot my brother?" Lydia's words came out harsh and quick.

Matthew's stomach hit the floor. Every nerve in his body trembled. "Calm down. Here, sit." He pointed to a chair in front of his desk.

"I'm not here to sit and chat. Just answer the question." She stared during his silence. "I guess by not answering, that tells me what I came here for." She grabbed the doorknob to leave.

"Lydia, wait. I can explain."

"Explain? Explain? How do you explain killing my brother, an unarmed man?" She whirled around, her eyes a mixture of anger and pain. "And how could you not say anything about it? Did you think I would never find out?"

That's exactly what he'd hoped. Now his worst nightmare was occurring. The woman he had grown to love stood before him, hate in her eyes.

"I'm sorry. I should have told you." Matthew folded into the chair he had offered her seconds before. All his energy drained. "You were just going through so much already."

Lydia ran a hand under her right eye. "Sorry just doesn't quite cut it in this situation." She turned and marched out the door.

Matthew rose to follow, but Sheryl took him by the arm.

"Don't." Her eyes held sorrow. "You should have told her."

Matthew pushed past Sheryl and rushed to catch Lydia as she raced out the front door. He hated the look of pain in her eyes.

"Lydia, please wait." He caught up as she reached the car.

"I thought I could trust you," she said. "I can't help but wonder what other secrets you're hiding from me."

Grabbing both her arms above the elbows, he turned her and forced her to look at him. "Lydia, I have only one secret. I'm crazy about you. Sometimes I catch just a brief glimpse of you, and it's all I can do to remember to breathe." It killed him to have caused her such pain. "I'm sorry I chose not to tell you about Charlie. It was stupid of me, but as time rolled on, the more I grew to care for you, fear of losing you kept me from saying anything."

She remained silent, her eyes narrow, as he tried to make her understand.

"We can work through this," Matthew pleaded. "I know we can." He glimpsed Sheryl walking to the passenger side of the car.

"How do we work through the fact that you shot and killed my brother? Do you honestly think I can ever forget that?" She pushed away, dropping into the driver's seat.

Matthew stared after her. He swore his heart crashed through his ribcage and landed on the ground with a thud.

LYDIA BRUSHED THE TEARS from her eyes. How could she have fallen for the man who killed Charlie? She picked up the phone, then placed it back down. Should she call and tell them? What if it brought back all those sad memories? At least she hadn't told them about the phone calls. That was one less thing for them to deal with. Maybe she should just keep it to herself. But how can she? This was a secret she couldn't keep. She picked up the receiver and dialed the number.

"Hello," her mom answered.

"Mom."

"Darling. How are you?"

"Not too good." She tried to force back the sob.

"What's wrong?"

"It's about Charlie. I met the man who killed him."

"You did."

"In fact, he's the new minister." She hoped by telling her mother it wouldn't bring all her pain back to the surface. She lowered herself into a chair in her dining room. Silence held on the line. Lydia had no words to offer for comfort. Her heart had broken into a million pieces. How was she to help her mother through this?

"We know," her mother said.

Lydia's heart jumped to her throat. "What do you mean *you* know?"

"Honey, before we gave our approval to appoint him, we did a thorough background check."

"And you still allowed him to take over the church? After what he did to Charlie?"

Her mother released a sigh. "At first, we were mortified. But the more we researched him, the more we realized he was the man God wanted to lead the church."

"But why didn't you tell me?" A sob escaped from Lydia. "At least prepare me for it?"

"We told you to look into the candidates before a new minister was chosen. You didn't want to be involved. You just kept saying God would put the right man in charge. Maybe we should have said something, but you had every chance to investigate his past as well. Besides, we wanted the people in the area to decide whether they wanted him to be minister based on him, not what he'd done in the past."

Lydia didn't know what to say. Her world was falling apart, and her parents could have prevented the whole situation.

"So, is he a good minister?" Her mom's voice was low.

"Yes, he's a good minister, but he's also the man who killed Charlie. He shot my brother. Your son." Lydia rose and paced the room.

"What else?"

Lydia paused. "What do you mean?"

"Do you honestly think we wouldn't have heard that you were dating him?"

"And you still didn't tell me?" She couldn't decide whose betrayal was worse, her parents' or Matthew's.

"If you two were meant to be, then it had to be your decision. Now, tell me about him? Better yet, tell me about you and him."

The floodgates released as Lydia spoke of her feelings for Matthew. "I really thought I cared for him. How could I when he did what he did?"

"Lydia, I loved your brother with all my heart. I remember when he was just starting middle-school. He had such hope, promise. But by the time he'd started high school he was different."

"Different? What do you mean?"

"Do you remember the summer before he started his freshman year, we told you he had to go to camp? You were mad you didn't get to go."

"I didn't think it was fair." She recalled her anger upon waking one morning and discovering Charlie was gone. All her dad would say was he would be gone all summer to a camp in Utah.

"It wasn't really a camp. It was a drug rehabilitation center. We were trying to get him free from the drugs."

Lydia grabbed hold of the table, sorrow filling her at not knowing the depths of her brother's addiction. "Was he really that bad at such a young age?"

"Yes. As time went on, it got worse. He was stealing and hurting others. And you're the one who told us that he got Jimmy hooked on drugs. We tried several other options, even a boot camp, but nothing seemed to work. No matter how we tried, the drugs just wouldn't let go of him. When we discovered he was selling to other teens, that was the last straw."

"That's no reason for him to have died. I overheard you and Dad say he wasn't even doing anything wrong when he was shot." Lydia's heart ached for the brother she remembered.

"We don't know what he'd been doing. To be in that alley in the first place meant he was up to no good. His shooting was an accident. I came to terms with it years ago. I've forgiven everyone involved, including your brother." Her mother let out a sigh. "Ask yourself, is this minister of yours really the type of man who would kill someone and be able to walk away? Or was it something that tormented him?" She paused, then added. "Also, don't forget, God wants us to forgive others."

"But how do you forgive someone who not only killed your brother but basically lied about it?" Lydia smashed a tear crawling down her cheek.

"That, my dear, is something you and God have to deal with together. I wish I could offer more help, but that's the best I can do." She sighed. "We have a few things we're committed to here, but we'll be up there in a couple of weeks. We'll discuss it then. If you need me or your father before, you can call or come down and stay with us so we can talk."

Lydia declined the offer of a visit. The conversation did little to offer her any peace. After hanging up, Lydia prayed for God to help her understand how both Matthew or her parents could have kept her in the dark. No matter how hard she tried, anger sat in the pit of her stomach.

MATTHEW HAD GOTTEN no sleep the night before. The angry look in Lydia's eyes raced through his mind. She had every right to be mad.

First thing that morning, he drove to Ringgold. He hadn't told his family about the shooting, and he knew there would be questions as to why he and Lydia were no longer together. It was better if they heard it from him.

"You should have told her, son." Dad said, seated in the plush recliner. "It might have saved you both some heartache."

"I know. I didn't feel the need at first. Then the more I fell for her, the less I wanted to lose her." Matthew leaned forward, his elbows on his legs. It had taken the rest of his strength to face his family with his secret. But he felt it was better to get everything out in the open. Hiding had gotten him nowhere.

"But that's exactly what happened."

Matthew plopped back. "It just never seemed like the right time." His heart ached.

"Knock it off," Brenda said. "You had no intention of telling her. You hoped she'd never find out. We're your family, and you didn't tell us. So, you can sit here and do the woe-is-me nonsense all you want, but you and I both know this is your fault, pure and simple." Brenda crossed her arms over her chest. "I can only imagine how poor Lydia feels."

Matthew stared at his sister. So much for support and kindness, even if was true. She was his sister. She should be on his side.

"You might never have a relationship with Lydia after this. But you have another problem to contend with." Brenda stood. "How long do you think it's going to take that Newman guy to see to it you're fired? I'd be coming up with a good sermon about the virtues of being honest before you find yourself out of a job." Brenda turned and marched from the room.

Matthew knew she was right. But at the moment, he wasn't sure he wanted to continue in Lincolnville. The prospect of bumping into Lydia at least once a week and seeing the hate held in her eyes might be too much torment.

LYDIA SURVEYED THE primer on the wall. It had taken two coats before they fully covered the discoloration on the wall. The cleaning crew Riley had sent over did the best they could at covering the blood, but stains shadowed through on the white walls.

"I saw Matthew yesterday." Sheryl stood back and reviewed her work. "He's as miserable as you are."

"He should have told me about Charlie." Lydia diverted her attention by repainting a spot-on a nearby floorboard.

"It's been three days. You need to stop torturing him, and yourself. At least talk to him."

Lydia let out a loud breath. "There's nothing to say."

"What happened to Charlie is probably not something he likes to talk about. You know what kind of person Matthew is. It must have been hard for him to shoot an innocent man."

Her mother's words rushed back to her. Was Matthew the type of man who could shoot an innocent man and walk away? Even in his days of being with the DEA? Each time Lydia asked herself those questions, she came up with the same answer. No. An ache lay deep inside her chest. It didn't help that she considered finding a new church to keep from bumping into him.

Sheryl wiped her forehead, leaving a trail of dull white. "How about we break for lunch while we wait for the paint to dry?"

"I appreciate you coming over. Doing this alone would have been hard." Lydia couldn't wait to apply the soft green color. The description at the store claimed the color gave peace and comfort. She could use some.

"Have you heard from Warren?" Sheryl asked.

"Except for his texts, there's been nothing."

"Maybe he forgot all about us."

"It could be he's just wrapped up in his new life. It's good for him to be away, meeting other people."

"If you say so." Sheryl smacked dust from her pant legs. "We've got more shopping to do. You still haven't replaced your bedspread." Sheryl placed the roller in a nearby paint pan. "We can also get some new accessories while we're out."

"I guess the bare walls look pretty bland." Lydia picked up the snapshot of Justin from the dresser in the hallway. The frame had been unsalvageable; however, she had the photograph repaired at a local studio. "How about lunch first, then we can go shopping?"

"Mail call." Sheryl announced as they walked outside. "A gift in a small box. Maybe it's a present from Matthew. It looks like jewelry. That's one way to get a woman to forgive you."

Lydia picked at the brown paper surrounding the box. There was no return address on the package. She hoped Matthew hadn't sent her a gift. It was better if he moved on with his life. She hesitated, contemplating opening it later, but knew it would only weigh on her mind for the rest of the day. Better to get it over with. She pulled the tape, releasing one side.

Sheryl bit her bottom lip while looking at the box. "I can't believe how slow you're going. Most women would rip it open."

Lydia got through the brown paper to a small white box inside. She sucked in a deep breath and opened the box. It dropped from her hand. A scream stuck in Lydia's throat as a bloody finger rolled across her porch.

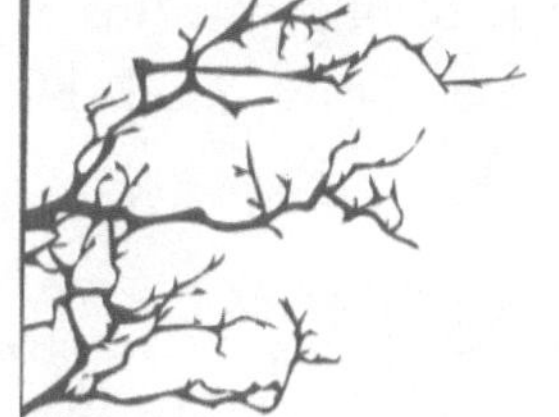

17

Matthew pulled in front of the white stone building behind two police cars and a white Chevrolet Malibu he recognized as Sheryl's car. He paused before entering. How angry was Riley at not knowing about his involvement in Charlie's death? Would he berate Matthew or listen to the circumstances before deciding on his guilt?

Phone calls to the church had been divided. Phyllis scolded him for not explaining the situation to Lydia beforehand. He could only imagine what Riley would say and expelled a weighted breath before climbing from the motorcycle.

Matthew stopped short upon seeing Lydia and Sheryl sitting with the sheriff through the glass window. Both women were pale as they talked.

"What's going on?" Matthew used his head to point as he spoke to Deputy Green.

"Seems someone mailed a finger to Ms. Frederickson."

The air flew out of Matthew. She must be terrified, yet she sat, stone-faced, as if willing herself not to show any emotion. Her jaw was tight, and she nodded instead of speaking.

Riley rose and walked from his office. "I'm going to have to forego lunch today."

Matthew nodded. "I heard." He glanced at Lydia. "How's she holding up?"

"As well as can be expected. According to the lab, it's the tip segment of a male pinkie finger."

"Do you know who it belongs to?" A sick feeling rose inside Matthew. He had a guess, and his instincts were always good. He prayed he was wrong.

"Not yet. There are no prints in AFIS."

"Is there any way you can get fingerprints for Warren Anniston to check against that pinky?" Matthew stared at Lydia, hoping his love for her didn't seep through his shirt.

"Warren. Why him?"

"It's pretty clear from this you aren't the target. If so, you'd have received the box, not Lydia. She's who this maniac's after." Matthew had to fight to turn his attention from the brunette.

"I thought Warren was in Seattle," Riley said.

"Last I heard, neither Lydia nor Sheryl have talked with him. They've only received texts. I also phoned my friend he was to stay with. He hasn't heard from him either. Just figured he'd made other plans."

"And going after a close friend would hurt her tremendously." Riley's voice became barely audible.

"I suggest you check Warren's blood against the sample you obtained from her wall."

He was grateful Lydia was in the other office and couldn't hear him. How would she react if Warren died as a way to hurt her? It might be enough for her to shut herself away and never come out. His eyes met hers. Pain showed in her expression. He couldn't be sure if it was from the stalker terrorizing her, or the hurt he'd inflicted.

Deputy Green answered the ringing telephone on the desk next to Matthew. "Sir, it's Anderson out on the north end. He says he needs to speak with you. Claims it's important."

Riley snatched the phone.

"What is it, Anderson? Well, I'll be. I'm on my way." After hanging up, Riley let out a breath of relief. "You're not going to believe this. Two fishermen near Water View Park found some guy wondering around.

He's been beaten up, and part of his finger's missing. He says his name's Warren Anniston."

LYDIA WAITED IN THE hallway outside the hospital room as Riley questioned Warren. She tried her best to ignore Matthew as he stared down at her from the opposite wall. She needed to shut off her feelings for him. Too bad her heart wasn't listening.

"I can't wait until I find out who did this. Nobody messes with Warren." Sheryl brushed tears with each angry word. "I've been taking care of him since I can remember."

Lydia pulled Sheryl closer to her, remembering when they first met Warren in elementary school. He'd been a small child, so the bigger boys picked on him. Sheryl had taken a liking to him and became his protector.

When the door opened, Lydia blinked back to the current situation. A reality she no longer wished to contend with.

"He doesn't remember a thing," Riley said. "The doctor says that's to be expected. He's dehydrated and has a nice knot on his head. There's a bit of hypothermia also. If he'd been hit any harder, they'd have never come across him." Riley glanced at Lydia, explaining in a low tone. "He could have stayed unconscious and died from exposure."

Sheryl let out a whimper.

Lydia hugged her tighter.

"Can we go in now?" Sheryl stood.

Lydia hesitated. Would Warren want to see her? After being held for weeks and beaten because he was her friend, she couldn't blame him if he held her responsible. She swallowed down the bile climbing through her system. She needed to get away from here. It would benefit not only her physical being, but her heart as well. It might also keep everyone she cared about safe.

"The doctor said not to stay too long, he needs rest," Riley said. "In a couple of days, he should remember more."

Tubes and wires ran from Warren's arms. The beeping of the blood pressure monitor was the only sound. Lydia had to smother a sob.

"Warren, are you all right?" Sheryl practically ran to his bedside. "Who did this to you? Who hurt you like this? You just let us know. Riley will lock them away, so they'll never hurt you again."

Lydia touched his arm above the IV. A bandage wound over his pinky down around his wrist on the other side.

"I'm sorry Warren. I'm so sorry." A welt grew in her throat as tears burned her eyes.

"It's not your fault." Warren whispered out the words. "Besides, it's probably better if I stayed here. I knew Sheryl would miss me if I'd really left."

Matthew paused upon entering, giving a sorrowful look. Lydia couldn't tell if it was because of Warren being hurt or their circumstances.

"Riley's left for the station. I wanted to check on how you're doing." Matthew leaned past Lydia and patted Warren on his shoulder. "I've already gotten some phone calls from other parishioners who want to know any way they can be of assistance."

"I appreciate that." Warren winced as he adjusted himself on the bed.

Lydia tried to halt the smell of Matthew's cologne invading her senses. As much as she wanted to fall into his arms for comfort, she wouldn't allow herself to do so. She not only still harbored anger toward him, but also knew no one was safe with this mad man haunting her.

"Once the doctor says Warren is strong enough to leave, I'm taking him to Savannah to look after him," Lydia said. "Once he's well, I'm going to take off."

"What's to stop this guy from following you?" Concern covered Matthew's eyes. "At least if you're here, Riley can have you protected."

Lydia pulled Matthew off to the side. She fought the palpitations of her heart at the touch of his arm. "I can't have anyone else I care about getting hurt. I can't take much more." Her tone lowered to a whisper. "I plan to take Sheryl along, and if I have to, I'll buy a gun."

"We have a great chance now of getting the person doing this." Matthew explained. "In a couple of days, after he's rested, Warren should be able to remember what happened. Then this nightmare will be all over."

A lone tear ran down Lydia's cheek. When would the nightmare of her broken heart end?

"You shouldn't run." Matthew said. "An agent I used to work with is coming to protect Sheryl." He brushed a strand of hair from Lydia's forehead. "She'll be one hundred percent safe. There's a guard posted out front of Warren's room, and no matter how much you fight, I plan to protect you."

A thought then popped into her mind—but who will keep you safe?

MATTHEW SLOWLY OPENED the door, looking in both directions as he went. He hoped some levity would help all those inside. Lydia and Sheryl stayed over with Warren while an officer stood guard outside. Visiting hours were in another hour. Both women looked up as Matthew tiptoed in. He put a finger to his lips, poking his head back out.

"Sh, I'm trying to avoid any disgruntled nurses." He referred to the nurse the evening before who threw everyone out except Lydia and Sheryl. "I'm on a special mission." Matthew over emphasized his steps and his shoes squeaked against the vinyl flooring. He stopped mid-step, contorting his face to the side, again searching the room, as if looking for someone to catch him before continuing.

Lydia's shoulders rose with each laugh. It gave Matthew hope she would forgive him, and they could move on with their lives.

"How's he doing?" Matthew stood next to Lydia's chair. His pulse beat in his ears as the aroma of her perfume glided over him.

"I'd be improving if these worry warts would stop hanging all over me." Warren opened his eyes. "It doesn't help that the nurses wake me every two hours to shove a pill in or take my blood pressure."

"Maybe this'll help." Matthew tossed the bag, hitting Warren in the chest.

"Betty's glazed donuts. My favorite." Warren stuck his nose in the bag and sniffed loudly. "The best smell in the world."

"Wendy Moreland suggested them." Matthew gave Lydia a wink. "She's asking about visiting with you."

"Tell her I'm fine and thanks." Warren lifted a donut, taking a bite. "Mmm. Good."

Matthew's cell rang. "It's Riley," he said as he looked at the caller I.D. He stepped a few feet from the bed and answered the call.

"I just wanted to let you know that box with the finger came from software parts from Computer Sense," Riley said.

"That's strange." Matthew turned his back on the other three. "One of his former co-workers, maybe?"

"That's not all. There's a cabin about two miles from the road where Warren was wandering around. It belongs to Donald Fisher, Warren's stepfather, and the owner of Computer Sense. We're bringing him in for questioning. Maybe you'd like to join us in an unofficial capacity."

"You bet I would." After hanging up, Matthew relayed what Riley had said.

"I knew Donald was mad about my leaving, but I can't imagine he'd go to these extremes." Warren looked at his missing fingertip before throwing the rest of his donut into the bag.

"Most of the people working for him are probably aware of that cabin," Matthew said. "Hopefully, we'll have some answers once Riley's done questioning him. I'll be over there if any of you need me. Pray something comes from it."

"Do me a favor. Take these two home first." Warren pleaded. "They're going to drive me crazy if they stay any longer. Besides, the doctor will be coming in soon, and they'll be taking me for some tests. It's ridiculous for them to sit around here waiting for me."

"Come on, ladies. You heard the man. Let's give him a break." Matthew ushered them toward the door.

Lydia leaned over and kissed Warren on his cheek. She then turned to Matthew. "Call as soon as they're done with Mr. Fisher."

"I will." Matthew pointed to Sheryl. "Ty Davenport, a former co-worker, is on his way to your place. He's one of the best, so you won't have to worry about anything happening. Just stay put until he arrives."

"Is he cute?" Sheryl smiled.

Warren rolled his eyes.

"I'm not the best judge on that, but he's extremely married."

"Couldn't have gotten a single man, could you?" Sheryl stuck her lip out in a pout as she bent to kiss Warren goodbye.

"I'll keep that in mind if we find ourselves in this situation again. And as for you." He took hold of Lydia by the hand. "Go straight home, lock up, and don't answer the door. I'll call Riley and have one of his deputies meet you there. I'll pick you both up later to bring you back here." When Lydia opened her mouth to speak, he added. "No arguments."

She glared at him, but eventually nodded her agreement.

"I hope Riley gets to the bottom of this. It'll be so nice to be done with it," Lydia said. "I feel stagnant with everything that's happened."

"Once Warren remembers, this will all be over." Matthew noticed Lydia had yet to remove herself from his grasp. It gave him additional hope she was softening in her anger toward him.

"Thanks for bringing the donuts by," Warren said as the three walked toward the door.

"That was nice of you." Lydia smiled and touched his arm.

Matthew's knees weakened. He only hoped he could fix things with this woman he wanted to spend the rest of his life. However, he knew that wouldn't be possible if anyone else got hurt.

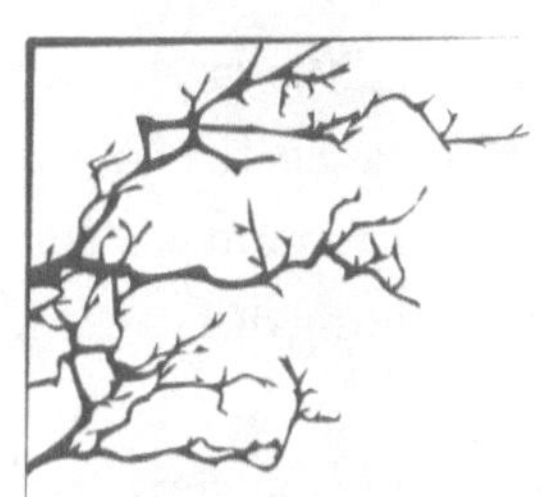

18

Matthew listened from the other side of the two-way mirror as Riley interrogated Donald Fisher. The man had a thin build, standing about five-foot-six. His pencil-thin mustache covered his upper lip, and his light-colored hair gave the appearance of being bald. Would he have been able to overpower Warren?

"First off, you're not under arrest." Riley opened a file on the table. "We need some information regarding the assault on Warren Anniston. We believe the same person is making threats to Ms. Frederickson."

Mr. Fisher leaned forward in his chair. "How can you be sure he isn't making it up?"

"The fact that the tip of his fingers has been cut off makes it highly unlikely."

"His finger? Oh, my. I thought that was only a rumor." Mr. Fisher's hand trembled as he placed it against his mouth. He grew pale. Fisher looked like he might faint before the interview even began.

"And they apparently kept him at your cabin in Water View Park." Riley is straightforward expression gave no hint of emotion.

"At my cabin?" He gasped and did a quick cross over his upper body. He then stared at Riley. "You think I did this? Is that why you called me down here?"

"We aren't sure who's responsible. I'd like to get your whereabouts for the past few days."

"Did Warren say I did this? If he did, he's lying. He's mad because I had to fire him."

Matthew stepped toward the two-way window. Warren hadn't mentioned being fired. That could explain why he'd taken the job in Seattle. He was probably ashamed and hoped it would remain a secret if he left. Too bad he didn't realize secrets had a way of being discovered, a lesson still fresh in Matthew's mind.

"Warren's memory's fuzzy. The doctor says it should be clear in a day or two," Riley responded. "A list of all your employees would be beneficial."

"Why would it be an employee of mine? Most people who live in the area know about my cabin." Mr. Fisher wiped at the sweat on his forehead. "Even James Newman and his son used it when they went fishing."

"There's this." Riley placed the white box that had previously held Warren's pinky on the table. "I believe this came from your firm. It was used to mail Warren's bloody finger to Ms. Frederickson."

Mr. Fisher's Adam's apple jumped as he examined the box through the plastic evidence bag. The finger was gone, but blood stains lingered.

"I'll drop the list off later this afternoon," he whispered.

"We appreciate that." Riley leaned forward. "And your whereabouts?"

"I'll give you an itinerary. I'll also ask my employees if there's been anything suspicious going on at the office." Mr. Fisher pushed himself from his chair. "You wouldn't expect this to happen in such a small town. It goes to show you, there's nowhere safe anymore."

Matthew walked from the room and joined Mr. Fisher and Riley in the hallway. "Mr. Fisher, I was listening in on your conversation with Riley. When the sheriff told you about Warren, you asked if he could have hurt himself. Why would you suggest that?"

Mr. Fisher glanced between the two men. "When I come back with the list of names, I'll also bring his computer."

Matthew and Riley watched Mr. Fisher as he walked out the door.

"I wonder what that's all about." Riley continued to stare after the man.

"Hard telling. Might be nothing." Matthew hesitated. "How's Lydia holding up?"

"Are you talking about the stalker or your involvement with Charlie?" Riley led as they walked to his office.

"Both." Matthew lowered himself into a chair.

"Better with her stalker than you. But she's not who you need to worry about. Her family's got a lot of pull in this area, and once they get with Newman, I imagine you'll be out of a job."

"I figured as much."

"Of course, I still have an opening, and I hire who I want." Riley sat in his chair and ran a hand through his hair. "What do you make of Fisher?"

"He's very knowledgeable about computers. Whoever is after Lydia would have to be technically savvy. However, Fisher went deathly pale when you showed him the box."

"It could be because his cabin and supplies were used. Can't be easy to take in."

"It could also be because he's afraid he's about to be discovered. It also bothers me that Newman is familiar with the area." Phyllis' words about Newman's attraction to Lydia rushed through Matthew's mind.

MATTHEW HESITATED BEFORE getting off the bike. He'd hoped he'd have some good news for Lydia after the interview with Fisher. Unfortunately, there hadn't been enough to hold him and no proof he'd been involved at all. Matthew's heart hurt as he walked up the stone walkway.

Would Lydia ever be able to forget what he did to her brother? His legs felt like they carried cement blocks as he walked to her front steps. How could he have been so stupid? He should have told her. He sucked in a deep breath and rapped on the door. The police car sat in front, but no officer was in sight.

"I'm almost ready," Lydia said upon opening the door. "Sheryl called and said your friend made it to her house."

"She'll be safe with him around." Her clean scent of gardenia filled the air. Matthew wanted to drown in the flowery scent.

"I hope so." Lydia paused and glanced around. Her eyes looked anxious, and a frown sat upon her face.

"What's wrong?" Matthew stepped inside. "Did you get another phone call?"

"No, I just had this feeling someone was in here with me earlier. There was a strange smell, and I thought I heard a noise."

"Where's the officer Riley sent over?"

"I don't know." She frowned. "I saw him walk around the house a while ago. Maybe he saw someone."

"Stay on the porch." Matthew walked around the downstairs inside Lydia's house. There *was* a strange odor. Almost medicinal. One she wouldn't recognize, but he did. *Chloroform.*

He returned to find Lydia standing in the doorway, a concerned look in her eyes. He hated to tell her the truth, but he didn't want another secret between them.

"I think you're right. Someone was here. There's dirt from a boot print inside your back door." He glanced at her feet. "I don't imagine you wear that large of a size."

"I think I'll stay at the hospital until Warren gets out. Between the guard Riley posted, the nurses and doctors running in and out, there'd be too many people for anyone to try anything."

"That might not be a bad idea. Maybe you can also stay with Sheryl for a day or two. She's got Ty, so you should be safe there." Matthew glanced up at the sky. While clear, it was still chilly out. "Why don't you put on something heavier? The weatherman mentioned the possibility of snow."

"I'll call Riley and let him know about our missing deputy." Matthew knew most officers would call it in if they'd seen something. "Don't worry. We'll figure out who this is."

After hanging up from Riley, he waited while Lydia grabbed her coat. "Riley's sending Deputy Green over. He asked us to wait outside." He led her to the motorcycle. While waiting for Deputy Green to arrive, Lydia took hold of Matthew's arm.

"I want to know about my brother," she said.

"What do you want to know?" Matthew felt a stone drop into the pit of his stomach. He swore he heard it echo when it hit. But after all he'd done, he owed her this much.

"Everything."

He stared into her eyes and saw pain. If knowing helped relieve some of it that was the least he could do. He leaned back on the motorcycle.

"I was working undercover and had infiltrated a motorcycle gang responsible for bringing drugs into the Miami area. The goal was to catch the guy bringing them into the country. Charlie was part of the gang."

"A big part?"

Matthew let out a heavy breath. This was going to be harder than he realized. "We're not exactly sure what his part was. He joined before I came along. His position wasn't very high. I never saw him hurt anyone though. He just dealt."

"Giving drugs to people is hurting them. Look at Jimmy." She crossed her arms over her chest. "Don't sugarcoat any of this to spare my feelings. I want to know the truth."

Matthew nodded and looked at the ground, hoping to make it easier. "We'd finally got the guy who was flying in a private jet, bringing drugs from Columbia. The meeting went down in an alley in Miami. After the bust, another crew of agents arrived. They separated the group between those violent and those considered not. They hoped the nonviolent ones would testify if given a reduced sentence. Three guys and a couple of girls were standing off to the side. Charlie was one of them." A shudder crossed over Matthew as he recalled that day.

"Was he handcuffed?" Lydia asked.

"No. He was standing by his bike and not considered a flight risk, so they hadn't cuffed him." Matthew let out a long breath. "They should have followed procedure."

"What happened next?" Lydia bit down on her bottom lip.

"One of the new agents saw him going into his pocket. He pulled out something shiny. The rookie yelled he had a gun. It turned out to be a lighter." Matthew ran his hand down his face. "It was the first time in my seven-year career I wished I'd missed."

"What happened to you?" She wiped at a tear straggling down her face. "Were you punished for killing him?"

"By the DEA, no. They ruled it an accidental shooting. The rookie got reprimanded and sent back to training. He eventually got a desk job. He was pretty shaken up, and he'd never trust his instincts again. Dangerous for him and other agents."

Lydia said nothing. She stared straight ahead, her brow furrowed.

He lifted himself from the bike when Deputy Green pulled up.

"I left the agency after that," he said before Green joined them. "I couldn't be sure it wouldn't happen again, and I couldn't take the chance of killing another innocent kid." A release came over Matthew's soul at telling her the story. It felt good to get it off his chest.

Matthew remained silent as Deputy Green went into the house. He returned within minutes.

"I took pictures of that boot print," the deputy said. "I'm not sure if anything will come of it, but we'll give it a try. Jones isn't responding to my calls. I'll look around and see if he isn't off eating someone's homemade cookies. No point in you staying. I'm sure it's nothing. I'll catch up with you later."

"Thank you." Lydia kept her eyes on Green as he walked around the side of the house. She turned to Matthew, her face still stone and her voice low and tense. "I guess we'd better go."

Green's lack of concern bothered Matthew, but that might be the way small towns did things. He climbed on the motorcycle. Lydia waited until he started it to get on behind him. His heart raced when her arms encircled his waist. They had a twenty-minute drive to the hospital. He loved the feeling of her holding on to him and he wished it could be like this always.

THE SEDAN CAME BEHIND them faster than he realized. A teenage driver, probably texting. There was no shortcut to the hospital, so Matthew had to take the old highway.

He swerved into the other lane to avoid being hit. The car followed. Matthew accelerated, avoiding the near collision. The speedometer read sixty. On the curve running to Lomax, he checked his speed again: sixty-five. The car had to slow at the curve. One more turn, and he'd catch a side road and lose it. The car inched up on the straightaway.

Lydia tightened her grip. Matthew prayed as they came to the next curve. As he rounded it, he crossed the lane to stay the momentum. A fallen tree blocked the road. He had no choice. He had to go off.

The bike hit a ditch and rose in the air before sliding across the ground. It spilled over several times. Matthew was thrown clear on the first tumble. He removed his helmet and shook his head to get his bearings. Lydia lay a few feet away on her side. She wasn't moving.

"Lydia."

She rolled over, sat up, and removed the black helmet.

"Are you all right?" Matthew scooted over to her.

"Yeah. How about you?" Lydia rose to her feet and brushed dirt from her jeans.

Bang!

Birds overhead flew from the branches. The shot echoed in the air.

"Get down!" Matthew shoved Lydia behind a large oak tree.

She glanced around. "I don't' see him." She pulled out her cell. "No signal."

Another loud blast reverberated in the cold air.

Matthew jerked back from the blow. Pain seared through his right shoulder.

"Matthew!" Lydia touched Matthew's cheek. Concern filled her eyes. "The lodge is about two miles over the hill. There's a first aid kit and other supplies. Also, a working phone."

Blood soaked his shirt beneath his jacket. It was cold against his skin. Pain ran through his arm. He hoped he didn't go into shock.

"Can you make it?" She had yet to remove her hand from his face.

He nodded and lifted himself from the ground. She wrapped her arm around his waist and helped him up the hill.

Another shot!

This one was farther away. Matthew hoped that meant the shooter didn't follow. He promised he'd protect Lydia. Unfortunately, with the loss of blood, he wasn't sure how much longer he would be conscious and able to keep that vow.

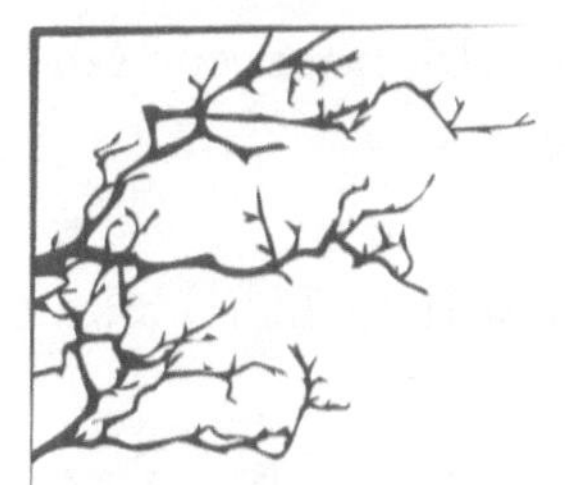

19

Snow fell in big white flakes. Normally the sight would excite Lydia, but right now, snow was the last thing she needed. A chill ran through her, though she wore a heavy wool coat. Her heart wedged in her throat as she prayed the maniac wasn't following them.

The lodge was only about a mile and a half over the hill. As Lydia stood on her tiptoes, she could see the chimney of the main house.

Matthew leaned on her more now than when they first started. He had weakened from the trek up. Hopefully, going down would be easier. Matthew's breathing intensified, almost to a pant. She had to get him to a hospital.

When they reached the summit, she tried her cell again. No luck. "Do you need to rest?" She held Matthew around the waist. His left arm wrapped around her shoulder.

"No. I'm okay." His words came in spurts.

"Once we get through the woods, we'll hit the lodge."

He nodded. Sweat coated him, his face now a ghostly white. Every couple of steps, he'd grunt from the pain. She did her best to hold him up and guide him through bushes and trees.

They hit a slick spot, and Matthew lost his footing. He toppled over, taking her down with him. Lydia tried to stop her momentum as she slid down the hill. She hit the bottom hard. Her body ached from the cold earth.

"Matthew." She crawled to him. He was breathing, but his eyes were closed. A scratch etched across his forehead. She wiped the blood with her finger. "Matthew, wake up. Don't give up now. How can I fight for us alone?"

175

His eyes crawled open. "You're not alone. We're together. And God is always with us."

"I forgot to tell you, I'm worth fighting for."

"Yes, you are." He let out a weak laugh. "I just thought I'd take a shortcut."

"Next time, let me know. I'll meet you at the bottom." She placed her hand on the side of his cheek. It didn't appear he had a fever.

He raised his hand up and touched her face. Warmth rushed through her. Try as she might to deny it, she had deep feelings for him. His pain when he spoke of her brother's death showed he ached over the shooting. She knew he wasn't the type of man to take killing someone lightly, whether in the line of duty or not.

"I'm sorry I hurt you." His voice rasped.

"Don't talk. You need to save your strength."

"Go on without me." His thumb caressed her lips.

"I won't leave you out here, alone." Tears blurred her vision. "Please Matthew, don't..."

"You'll be okay." He patted her arm. "Go on. Get help."

Lydia fought tears wanting to fall. "It's not that far. I'll be back in a few minutes. You hang on." She shoved off her coat and covered him with it. She rose, took a step, then stopped and looked back.

Matthew stared at the sky. His palms were together, and his lips mouthed words she couldn't hear.

"That's right, pray," she whispered as she walked away. "Between God and me, you'll make it." Her walk turned into a run.

LYDIA'S CHEST HURT when she burst through the last patch of trees. A cabin connected to the lodge stood within feet. She rushed to the front porch and jiggled the knob. It was unlocked.

She raised her eyes to the sky. "Thank you, God."

She recalled the bathroom was just past the small kitchen and ran to it. Inside, she found a mess. Blood covered gauze strips littered the floor. Where did they come from? It didn't matter, not right now. She had to focus on getting help for Matthew. She tore through the drawer, looking for the first aid kit.

She found the kit, then ran to the first bedroom and tugged the quilt off the bed. Next would be the main house where she hoped the phone was working.

Patchy sun cascaded through the window, casting a yellow glow into the room. Her peripheral vision caught sight of a picture hanging on the wall. Several pictures, in fact. Each were held up with tacks. Some were her wedding pictures, some in the park, and also one at the rest area with Matthew. She gasped, glancing from photograph to photograph. Justin's and Matthew's faces were no longer beside her. Instead, another man had taken their place.

At once, she sensed his presence. She straightened, frozen in place. He was within inches. The smell of antiseptic attacked her senses.

"Are you enjoying my collection?"

She spun. "Warren. What are you doing here?"

She couldn't immediately make it register. Her mind raced. The pictures, the bloody gauze in the bathroom. She inhaled, suppressing the dread inside. Icy fear trailed down her spine. She worked to steady her expression, not wanting to give way to the terror inside.

After a brief pause, she said, "I'm so glad you're here. Someone tried to shoot me. He hit Matthew instead."

"Where is Matthew?"

She looked out the small four pane window. Flakes of snow fell harder. "Out there." Tears welled. "I'm scared."

"Don't worry. You're safe with me, and we don't need to worry about Matthew anymore." Warren's finger stroked her cheek.

A chill edged up her body as if an ice pick ran along her back.

"I've waited a long time to have you," he said. "You'll make me very happy." He brought his mouth toward her.

"No, Warren." Lydia pushed him away. "I haven't got those feelings for you. I consider you a friend, a brother."

"I am *not* your brother, and I'm tired of being the one who makes you laugh." He shoved her, and she fell into a nearby dresser. "Can't you see I'm devoted to you since we were kids? I would move Heaven and Earth for you."

She straightened. "I also care about you, but we're not in love." Her mind raced with thoughts of what could be wrong to cause Warren to act in such a way.

"Look at us. How can you say that?" Warren pointed to the images on the wall. "Look how happy we were."

What was his problem? Was he playing some game? Anger rose inside her. How could he not see she was upset? This wasn't like Warren at all.

"These aren't real. You manipulated them on your computer." Lydia ran to a wedding portrait, tearing it from the wall. She continued destroying snapshots, yelling with each. "This isn't you, it's Justin."

"That's me with you. When I was the man you loved."

"Stop it. That's not us. We were never married. I married Justin. I loved Justin." She finally came to a photo with Matthew. Pulling it from the wall, she tore Warren's picture from it. "And this, this is of Matthew and me at the rest area outside of Lincolnville. I love Matthew, not you."

The words tumbled from her mouth. Until that moment, she hadn't realized it herself. It shocked her to a standstill. She loved Matthew.

"Don't say that. Don't say his name. Not here. He doesn't belong here." Warren grabbed her above her elbow so hard she winced. Madness gleamed in his eyes, and a sneer ran across his lips. "We were happy until he interfered with us. But I forgive you. And now it's only you and me. We can be happy again, like we used to be. See how much I love you. That's why I forgive you."

"Forgive me for what?" Lydia jerked away. "I haven't done anything wrong except maybe in your mind. I loved Justin. You were there as I watched him slowly die. You know how much I loved him." She hesitated. "And now, I *love* Matthew."

"Shut up!" He grabbed her by the neck and shoved her against the wall. "If you ever say that name again, you will have to be punished. You wouldn't want that. Would you?"

"No." The word barely came out a whisper as Lydia stared at him. She fought to halt hysteria from grabbing hold. His features were that of a person she didn't recognize. She'd never seen those cold dark eyes in her good friend before now.

Warren grabbed her by the upper arm and dragged her to the living-room. All the while, Lydia tried to persuade herself that he'd never hurt her. It must be the bump on his head causing this craziness. There has to be something wrong with his brain. That could be the only explanation for his strange behavior. But it had to have taken a while to make the pictures.

A fire in the fireplace warmed the room, and he stopped to light candles on the mantle.

The harder Lydia tried to deny it, the more she realized he must have been the person terrifying her. He knew her routine. He'd been in her house pretty much every day, even having a key to all her locks, new and old. Riley said it was someone using a computer. Warren's expertise. All the pieces fit.

She cringed. Had he been altering the pictures over years or just recently? It was hard to tell.

"You've got to see it, how much I want you." Warren's words came out bitter as he punched at the logs in the fire with a poker. "Everything has been to show you that."

"You never let me know." She eased herself into an oversized chair. The warmth of the fire reminded her of Matthew out in the cold. She had to help him. He couldn't die.

"How could you not notice?" He jabbed harder. Sparks flew into the air. "If you cared, it would have been obvious."

"I've never had quite that presence of mind when it came to men." Lydia folded her hands, praying God would make a way through to her friend and for someone to find Matthew.

"Except when it came to Justin." Warren's jaw set tight as his expression iced over. "And that new preacher."

"Why didn't you just say something? Why scare me with the phone calls?" She asked to confirm her suspicions.

"You were supposed to call me. I would have saved you. But no, Sheryl had to insist on calling Riley. All because she has the hots for him. She shouldn't have done that." His voice lowered. He rose and leaned on the mantel, pulling a knife from his belt. He stabbed the knife into the wood. It now stood erect. "She'll discover the punishment for being so nosey."

No! Lydia inwardly screamed. "Did you tell her about your feelings for me?" She willed herself to remain calm. Glancing out the window, she was grateful to see it had stopped snowing.

"Are you kidding? She would have told the whole town. Everyone would have known before you."

"Then why are you mad at her?" Lydia said. "You know she's wrapped up in her own little world. She shouldn't be blamed. The only other people she cares about are you and me."

"That might be true, but she shouldn't have kept pushing the preacher onto you. If she hadn't been such a busybody, this wouldn't have happened."

"If you kept quiet, it's your fault." Lydia's tone was more forceful than she felt. How could she not know Warren loved her? How could she not see his instability? She scolded herself for not being aware of him coming apart. "I'm sorry." She whispered. A tear rolled from her lashes. "Justin's death hurt so much I didn't want to see or feel anything at the time."

"That's why this is perfect." He walked over to her and knelt beside the chair. "You and me. Justin's no longer between us. We can be together. Everything I did, I did for you."

"Crank calls and messing up my house don't really say love."

"I'm taking about Jimmy."

"Jimmy?" Lydia mentally pinched herself, hoping to wake from this nightmare.

"I wouldn't let him get away with hurting you anymore." Warren's voice was calm and indifferent to the fact he had killed a man. "I protected you."

"*You* killed Jimmy?" Lydia's chest rose and fell from the trepidation. "Whose blood was on the walls?"

"Mine, of course. I knew the cops would test it." He walked over to the large sofa across from her and plopped down. "I figured if I was hurt, you'd realize how much you cared for me."

"I do care for you. I just don't love you like a woman should love a man."

"But I've always adored you." He held up the partially amputated fingertip. "I did this for you. I'll bet your preacher wouldn't hurt himself to show how much he cared."

Lydia fought the bile rising in her throat at his sick fantasy. How could he have kept this insane persona hidden so well? His facial features were even different. He held a twisted expression with cold, uncaring eyes. His jaw set in place as he constantly ground his teeth.

"You shot the old man at the rest area." The words barely escaped her lips.

"I only tried to scare you." He paused. A sneer ran across his lips. "I should have dispatched Matthew to the great beyond then and there. It would have saved quite a bit of trouble. I figured when you found out about Charlie, you'd never want to see him again."

"You knew about Charlie?"

"When you started dating Matthew, I researched him."

"Why didn't you tell me?" She jumped to her feet. Everyone had kept it a secret from her. Who else knew? "How could someone who claimed to care for me keep that a secret?" Anger was taking over her fear.

"You'd ask why I was checking up on him. Since I had no excuse, I e-mailed the information anonymously to James. I knew he'd take care of Matthew for me. It never dawned on me you'd ever forgive him for killing Charlie. You can't seem to stay mad at anyone for very long."

"That should make you feel good," she said. "It means once this is over, I'm likely to forgive you, too."

Warren laughed. "You really don't understand, do you? Since I can't have you in his world, I plan for us to spend all eternity together."

A rock dropped deep into the pit of her stomach and her hands trembled. In order to survive, Lydia knew she had to remain calm. Right now, she had to focus on getting away so she could save Matthew before he froze or bled to death. The words stuck in her mind. The temperature was already below freezing. She had to get to the main house and to the phone.

"How does your hand feel?" She inhaled her apprehension.

"It hurts." Warren placed the knife on the coffee table.

"We should put some ice on it." She pushed herself from the chair, praying her shaking legs could carry her. As she neared the freezer, Lydia spotted a broiler fork next to a dish towel on top of the counter. Feeling his gaze upon her, she pulled the ice tray out and released its contents into the sink. She angled her body just right so Warren couldn't see her hide the fork under the towel. She startled when he stroked her back. He took in a whiff of her hair.

"I wish it didn't have to be like this. But we'll enjoy each other once before it's over." While he stood with a hand on her back, the other with the missing tip rested on the countertop.

She yanked the fork out and jabbed the tines into his sore hand. He shrieked out in pain as she spun in the opposite direction. Warren fell to the floor. It gave Lydia a chance to jump around him. She darted out the door. After bounding from the steps, she raced toward the trees. Away from where she left Matthew to keep him from harm's way.

Her heart pounded so loud she could hear nothing else. Not her panting. Not her feet pounding against the ground. Or even Warren seconds before he tackled her. She screamed. Please let someone hear her. His hands wrenched her head back. Another scream escaped from her.

"You will never do that again." He then smashed her face into the snowy dirt.

Lydia's stomach swayed as he lifted her.

He spun her to face him. His eyes were wide with rage. "Do you think your preacher will want you after you've been with me?" Warren spoke through clenched teeth.

Lydia slammed her forehead against his nose. He released his hold. She landed on the ground, momentarily dazed by the blow she'd dealt. Warren turned back to her, and she raised her leg. With all her might, she kicked Warren in his kneecap. He fell to his side. She struggled to stand on the slippery ground. Warren grabbed hold of her ankle and pulled her back to him. His knee landed on her back and the air flew from her. He flipped her over and backhanded her several times. Tears rolled from the sting of the slaps.

"You will never leave me. Never!" His volume raised two octaves, making him sound like a frantic, hysterical female.

He hauled her from the ground and shoved her toward the lodge. As he propelled her forward, she darted in different directions. Any chance at freedom. Each time, he flung her back. The fight had almost left her. He dragged her back into the bedroom with the false images scattered on the floor. He gathered her hair in his hands and crashed her face into the wall. Blood slid down her throat.

MATTHEW SMELT GARDENIAS in Lydia's coat. He couldn't tell what warmed him more, the wool coat or the aroma. *Yeah, she was worth fighting for.*

He rose on his good arm and knees. It took work, but he forced himself to crawl to a nearby tree where he sat up. It took all his focus to unbutton his shirt. The blood seemed to have slowed. He leaned forward and reached over his shoulder. Blood covered his fingertips. Pain shot through his body. The shot penetrated his upper chest and went clean through.

"God, I'm going to need a lot of your help right now," he said to the clear sky above. It was dusk and would get dark soon. And colder. He needed to get inside.

With much effort and discomfort, he removed his jacket and shirt. He tied the shirt and placed it over his head. His teeth gritted as he lifted the arm into the makeshift sling. He then replaced his jacket. Now all he had to do was wait for Lydia. A smile crawled over his face. Wouldn't she be surprised to see him alive? He pushed his way up the bark of the tree until he stood. His hands shook and cold rushed through him with only bare skin beneath the jacket.

He sucked in a deep breath. Thank goodness the snow had let up. If Lydia hadn't left her coat, he would have had the chills.

Something in his side pocket moved. He removed the vibrating phone as he took a step to the next tree. His breath came out in gusts with every move.

"Hello." He cleared his throat. "Hello."

A scream in the distance diverted his attention. Lydia!

"Matthew? Where are you?" Riley's voice came in strong, but Matthew couldn't answer.

Another scream. He had to get to Lydia. He pushed through a large group of trees. Bushes smacked at him, but he didn't feel it. His total focus was on getting to Lydia.

"Please God. She is worth fighting for." He continually whispered the words as he made his way forward. His legs felt as if walking through quicksand.

He almost yelled out when he saw Lydia until he realized a man was shoving her back toward the cabin.

"Matthew!" The voice beckoned again over the line. He took a deep breath and raised it to his ear. "We're going to track you by way of your phone. Make sure you leave it on."

"No need." Matthew stopped to catch his breath. "I'm near one of the cabins at the ski lodge. I've been shot. It's Warren."

"We figured that. He's missing from the hospital. His guard is dead, along with the deputy guarding Lydia. Green found him in the woods. Both were stabbed."

"He's the one. Warren. Warren's the one responsible for it all." Matthew fell against a tree for support. His legs wobbled. It took all his strength to talk.

"On his work computer, we found pictures of Lydia where Warren superimposed his face over other people." Riley let out a heavy breath. "Where's Lydia?"

"He's got her. *He's* got Lydia."

20

Lydia's head and face hurt, but she couldn't dwell on the pain. Matthew had to be cold. She had to get out of here and get to that phone in the other building. She searched the room for a weapon. Tearing through the closet, she found more blankets. Nothing in the dresser drawers. She rushed to the window. It was nailed shut.

She would not let Warren win. She didn't want to hurt him, but he was no longer the friend she had grown to care for.

When she opened the nightstand, stationery and a pen beckoned to her. She prayed that someone found Matthew before it was too late for him. Her hands trembled as she wrote the quick note, but she hoped she made herself clear. Footsteps sounded in the hallway. She tossed the notebook into the safety of its drawer. Please God, let the message make its way to Matthew. scooted to the corner created by the bed and nightstand.

The door opened.

"How can you say you care for me and hurt me like you have?" Lydia said as Warren stood over her.

"Why couldn't you love me?" Warren's stone-cold expression stared back at her. "Why couldn't you just try to love me?"

"I told you I did. I'm sorry it can't be how you like."

"That's not enough."

"God wouldn't want you to do this. If we pray, we can find an answer before it's too late."

"God. Yeah. I prayed over and over for Him to let you notice me. You can't imagine how many times I asked Him to let me have you. Some God."

"How can you say that?" She climbed onto her feet. "You taught Sunday school, a sat in church every week, sang praise and worship. You're a Godly man, deep inside. I know you are."

"I believed for you. You would only marry a Christian man, so that's what I became."

"God doesn't always answer our prayers how we hope. Sometimes it isn't His will."

"I'm really not in the mood for a sermon."

Warren jerked her up by the shirt and dragged her to the fireplace. The living-room lay in ruins. Torn pictures strewn across the floor and shattered glass throughout. More photographs where he had superimposed himself over others now destroyed. Lydia's throat constricted when she saw her face melting in the flames of the fireplace.

LYDIA'S SCREAM STILL echoed in his ears. Matthew couldn't chance waiting for Riley. He had to get into that building. He slid around a pine tree, glancing in every direction. The palm of his hand hurt from having to use limbs to maneuver. Matthew had no choice but to move slow. Sheer determination gave him the momentum to persevere.

He crept across a twenty-foot opening. Resting his shoulder against the wood frame of the building, he sucked in a deep breath. Man, his shoulder hurt. *Don't think of the pain. Think of Lydia. She's worth fighting for. She's worth fighting for.* The words repeated in his head.

He edged up to the first window. A living-room area. Lydia sat in an oversized chair. Fear glossed her eyes. A bruise covered her left jaw, and her hair was no longer in a tight, neat ponytail.

Warren's head turned as if glancing around while he paced. His hand rose to his mouth every few seconds. He spoke, but Matthew couldn't make out the words.

Matthew's heart stopped when Lydia's eyes met his. She glanced at Warren, then back at Matthew. Her eyes deliberately moved to a nearby coffee table. Matthew followed her line of vision. A heavy gauge utility hunting knife, called a Skinner. He also knew Warren had a gun.

Matthew glanced around. Where was the car? If nothing else, a tire iron might be useful.

Matthew got down on his knees and crawled under the window. Once passed it, he moved toward the rear of the cabin. A black sedan was parked in back. He continued in a crawl until he got to the vehicle. He gave God a quick thanks for no alarm and an unlocked door. Matthew dug around under the driver's side seat. He felt a familiar grip as he pulled out the Beretta Tomcat handgun. Not good for a long distance, but up close, it'd work in a pinch. And you don't have to get as close as with a knife.

LYDIA CONTINUALLY GLANCED at the window for any sign of Matthew. Her heart still lay in her throat from when she first saw him. It took all her power not to call out his name. Did she tell him about the phone in the main house?

She got to her feet. If Matthew were anywhere near, she had to keep Warren distracted. "It's a good thing Justin died of cancer, or I would think you were to blame for that, too."

"I knew you loved him, and I could tell how much he loved you. If you were happy, that was fine. I loved you from a distance."

"But now that's changed?"

Warren fluctuated between reality and fantasy. One minute he thought he was the man she married. The next he realized it was Justin she had been married to. How was she going to get through to someone this unstable?

"When Justin died, you grew to rely on me. That's when I realized we were meant to be together. But then that preacher had to show up."

"I can't help my feelings. Any more than you can. If you had told me sooner, there might have been a chance. We might have been able to see if something might have ignited. But now it's too late." Lydia turned to face Warren. "I'm sorry Warren. Hurting me or anyone else won't change the way I feel."

She knew she was rambling, not even sure what she said made sense. "You just have to face facts and accept responsibility. And the phone calls started before Matthew came to town, so don't blame this on him. This is your fault. So, I suggest we quit all this, and you take me home."

"I don't think so. None of it matters anymore." He walked over to the coffee table and stared down at the knife. "We'll have one last night, then it'll be all over. I need to have you, just once."

"Even if it's against my will?" Lydia's pulse raced.

"You can either make it easy on yourself or hard. We both know I'm stronger, and I'll win."

The side door crashed open.

"Warren, it's all over." Matthew's hands shook as he pointed the gun at Warren.

Matthew moved to the opening of the hallway. Lydia's heart pounded in her chest. He was pale and sweat rolled down his face. She wanted to run to him, but she would have to pass Warren to do it. He was within feet of Matthew.

"Get away from the knife." Matthew ordered.

"Or what? You'll shoot me." Warren took a step toward Matthew. "She's just beginning to forgive you for Charlie. I'm not sure if she can forgive you for me."

"At least she'll be safe." Matthew motioned with the weapon for Warren to move aside.

"No. I can't imagine you'll shoot another unarmed man." Warren smirked. "From what I read in the reports, killing Charlie took a real toll on you mentally." He took another step toward Matthew. "Have you even held a gun in your hands since that day?"

Anger rose in Lydia. How dare he taunt Matthew like this over something that was an accident? Of course, it bothered Matthew. He was a good man. Matthew shook his head and swiped his arm across his face.

Warren raised his leg and kicked the gun from Matthew's hand. Warren then shoved him to the ground. The wince of pain showed all over Matthew's face. Lydia rushed at Warren, sending them both to the ground. She pounded on him with her fists. He shoved her sideways and rolled over on top of her.

"Now that your boyfriend's here, I say we let him in on some of the fun." Warren ground his lips into hers. He jerked back with a jolt from her bite, bringing his hand to his mouth.

"Get off me, now," Lydia growled.

Warren slapped her across her face, then rose, taking her with him. He held her by the hair and shoved her toward the other side of the room, near the fireplace. She landed hard on the floor.

Using one arm, Matthew scooted across the floor on his belly, his eyes on the gun. Warren landed hard with his knee on Matthew's right arm. A yell escaped Matthew's throat. He grabbed his injured arm and rolled onto his back.

Lydia had to find some way to stop this.

Warren stared down at Matthew. "I was going to let you watch me take her, but I think it's just better if she watches you die first."

With Warren's focus on Matthew, Lydia scooted toward the gun. *God, please let this be a bad dream. Either she and Matthew die, or Warren dies. That's not much of an option.*

Warren walked to the coffee table and picked up the knife. Lydia paused when he looked her way.

"I say we end him and get on with us."

Warren carried a smirk as he continued to glare down on Matthew. He didn't look back as her fingers curled around the cool metal of the gun.

Warren took another step toward Matthew. The knife reflected in the window. Matthew grabbed a pillow from a nearby chair. Each time Warren sliced at him, stuffing flew. Anger creased Warren's face and his mouth stood in a sneer as he swiped the knife back and forth.

"I'm done playing with you." He jerked the pillow from Matthew's grip and took a swipe. As Matthew raised his hand to block it, the knife sliced into his palm. Lydia gasped at seeing the blood. She closed her eyes and squeezed the trigger.

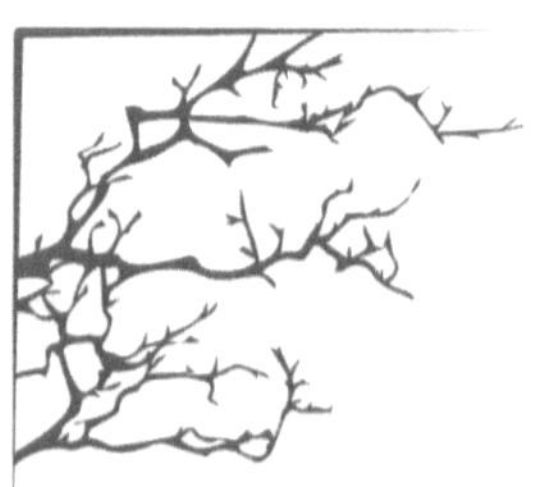

21

Matthew flinched at the boom of the gun in the small room.
Warren stood motionless for what seemed an eternity. The knife slid from his hand and his body folded over into a pile on the floor. The odor of gunpowder drifted in the air. On the other side of Warren sat Lydia, leaning against the fireplace. The Beretta in her grip. Her hands shook as tears flowed from her eyes.

Matthew crawled to her.

"It's all right. It's over." He removed the gun from her trembling hands.

"I didn't mean to," she cried. "I just wanted him to stop."

"I know. You had no choice." Matthew kissed the side of her face and brought her into his chest.

LYDIA SAT STUNNED. Her mind couldn't fathom what had happened. Did she *really* kill Warren? Or was it all just a bad dream? The proof stood all around her. Deputies, paramedics, and Riley whisked in and out of the cabin.

She looked over at Matthew being tended to by a paramedic. Blood covered his clothes. A white bandage surrounded his left hand. But the color had returned to his face. He was alive. The other paramedic brought in a gurney. She forced herself to her feet on wobbly legs.

"Are you sure you're all right?" Her voice sounded hollow through the ringing in her ears. The gun blast inside the room had been louder than expected. She grabbed his hand once the paramedics had him strapped down.

"I will be." He gave her hand a squeeze. "I'm sorry about everything."

She nodded.

Riley walked over and took her hand in his. "I'm sorry. We found pictures that Warren had manipulated on his computer. If we'd found them sooner, we might have been able to stop this. I'm just glad you're both all right."

Lydia fought the tears welling in her eyes. How could this not be a dream?

"Sheryl's on her way," Riley said to Lydia. "And an air ambulance is coming for you. We need to get that gunshot looked at." He patted Matthew's good shoulder.

Once outside, the cool fresh air slammed into Lydia. It was a stark contrast to the cabin.

Minutes later, the helicopter lifted, taking Matthew to Chattanooga, the closest trauma center. Blonde hair caught Lydia's attention and tears flowed when Sheryl raced from the police car. She took Lydia in her arms and held her while Lydia sobbed.

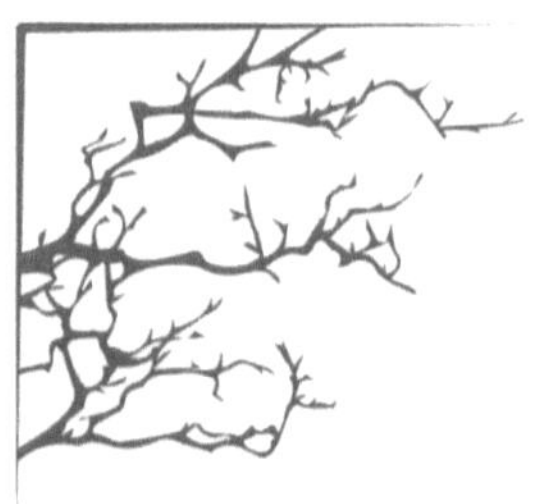

22

Matthew twisted and turned, trying to get comfortable. He hated hospital beds. They were too stiff.

The door opened, and Riley entered. "How're you doing?" He placed his hat on a side chair.

"I'll be fine once I get out of here," he said, though he knew he was too weak to care for himself. "How's Lydia?"

"Physically, she's fine. Emotionally, she's still on edge, but I guess that's to be expected." Riley pulled a chair up. "She should be back pretty soon."

Back? Had she been there, and he not known it? When the nurse woke him to take his vitals, the room was empty.

"She insisted on driving your dad home to get some rest, then she was stopping by her house for a quick shower and to change her clothes. You've been out for two days."

Matthew licked his dry lips. That explained why he'd awakened to find himself alone.

"During our search of the cabin, we found a journal Warren kept. He wrote about people who had done him wrong, whether real or imagined. Sheryl was on his hit list for pushing you and Lydia together, his stepfather for firing him, which in his mind would make Lydia feel less of him. He also put those cuts and bruises on himself." Riley hesitated. "It was a pretty elaborate scheme. He planned to kidnap Lydia, figuring no one would suspect him because he had moved across the country."

"He was a sick man."

194

"Justin never liked Warren. He never gave a reason and was too sick at the time for me to push for an answer. Now I wish I had."

"Warren was in love with her. I saw it. Maybe Justin did too. I just never thought he'd do anything to hurt her." It took all Matthew's energy to say the words.

"We also found this." Riley pulled out a piece of paper from his pocket.

Matthew recognized Lydia's handwriting. Just what he needed, a Dear John letter. His heart collapsed.

"It's only a copy," Riley said. "The original's at the station. I thought you'd like to see it. If you need anything, you let me know."

Matthew nodded and watched Riley leave. He then opened the folded note. Tears welled as he read the words.

MATTHEW:

No matter what happens, I wanted to tell you I'm sorry for everything that has occurred between us. I used every conceivable excuse not to fall in love with you, but it didn't work. I do love you. I also forgive you for Charlie. He was so far gone by the time you met him. I wish he'd had someone like you for a friend when he was a teen. Things might have turned out different. If I never see you again, I want you to know how much I care about you. I'll always love y

HE TOOK IN THE WORDS, letting them fill his body. He tucked the note beneath his pillow so it would be near for him to read again, and again, and again. A knock on the door drew his attention away.

"Come in."

Matthew had hoped for Lydia. Instead, James Newman, III walked in.

"Matthew, how are you holding up?" James wore a smile that said he'd put a knife in Matthew's back if he wasn't lying on it.

"I'm doing well. Doctor says the bullet missed all the vital stuff."

"Good. Good." James nodded and glanced at the ground. "I hate to be the bearer of bad news with everything else you've gone through, but the committee is meeting later today about your position. After finding out about you and Charlie, I'm not sure there's a chance you'll keep the job."

"That's their decision." Matthew wanted to knock the gloat from James' eyes.

"You really should have told us."

"Told you what?" He didn't have the strength to deal with this right now. "It's common knowledge on my record. I never hid anything."

"I know. It's just hard with Lydia and her family having so much influence in the church. I can only imagine what her father would say if he found out the minister we hired killed his son."

Matthew winced at his words.

"I know exactly what he'd say."

James spun to find Lydia standing behind him, her hands on her hips.

LYDIA WAS READY TO throw this man from a window. She didn't care if they were on the sixth floor. "My father would say that God obviously brought him here for a reason. And if the people on the committee are too stupid to see how important he is to this community, they don't deserve him."

James coughed, his jowls a shade of red. "I'm not too sure about that. A father's love is a powerful thing."

"Would you like to call him? I just spoke to him about it this morning. He plans to be at that meeting this afternoon to express his wishes." She walked up and took Matthew's hand in hers. "If you think you're going to throw Matthew out of that church, you'll have to fight me and mine to do it. And like you said, with the influence my family has, I don't think that'll be easy."

James stood opened mouthed. She'd left him speechless. Not an easy task when dealing with a politician.

"Now, if there's nothing further, I suggest you leave." Lydia gave the best stern look she could. It would have been easier if the heat from Matthew's touch wasn't interfering. "I have some important things to discuss with Matthew."

James said nothing further as he turned and marched out the door.

Matthew gave Lydia's hand a squeeze. "I guess I'm not the only ornery one around here."

"I have my moments." She sat on the side of the bed. "So, how are you feeling?"

"Wonderful now. How about you?" He reached up and touched the bruise on the side of her face. The color had gone from red the day before to purple.

"I'll be okay. I'm still having a hard time reconciling my feelings about Warren. We were such close friends." Tears welled in her eyes. "Sheryl and I discussed having a small ceremony for him."

"If you want, I'll officiate. Overall, I liked the man."

"I think that would be nice." Warmth filled her. She pushed hair from Matthew's forehead. "I had no idea Warren had those feelings."

"He hid it well." Matthew took her hand in his. "He had everyone fooled, maybe even himself."

"I should have known he was sick. We were supposed to be friends."

"He gave off the persona of a decent guy." Matthew kissed her palm.

"I took your dad home. He insisted on staying the night, but he was looking tired this morning. I was afraid he'd make himself sick." She grinned. "I think your sister's trying to make me fat. She had a large breakfast waiting when we got there."

"That's Brenda. Always enough to feed an army. Thank you for taking care of my dad."

"I told him you'd call if you woke up before he came back."

Matthew nodded.

"I was afraid I'd never see you again." Her hand now rested on the side of his face. He needed a shave, but she didn't mind the rough whiskers against her skin. "I thought you might die or freeze to death out there in the woods."

"But I didn't." Matthew pulled something from beneath his pillow. "Riley found your letter."

She wiped a tear that had slid from his eye. Her stomach bounced at what his reaction might be. Was it too soon for her to let him know?

"I was afraid I'd die without being able to tell you how much you meant to me."

Matthew combed his hand through her hair. "Your family might not be too happy about the fact I shot Charlie."

"My parents came to grips with it years ago. They knew about it before you were hired, yet they still thought you were the man for the job."

"Did you mean what you said about being in love with me?" He flipped open the note.

"Yes. I love you. Even if you don't feel the same, I wanted to let you know how much I appreciate you coming into my life. I know we've only known each other for a short time, but..."

He placed a finger over her lips. "I love you, too." He put his hand in her hair, brought her to him, and kissed her. "I'm ready to face anything that comes our way, especially with you at my side."

"I'll be there every step of the way."

THE END

Check out the next in the Lincolnville Mystery Series:

Catch Your Breath

Catch Your Breath
1

The woman stared leaned against the building across the street from the art shop. She glanced at the store every few seconds. Her jacket was different, but the cap was the same, and so were the suede boots. Calley Regan swore she was the same person she'd seen earlier. Besides, with the temperature in the upper eighties, why wear a jacket unless you were trying to hide?

"You noticed her too?" Her boss, Eva Martinez, placed her coffee mug in the microwave. She walked up and looked over Calley's shoulder. "I spotted her when I got in this morning. You don't think she's planning to rob the place or is a lookout for someone else, do you?"

"Not with those Cesare Paciotti boots." Calley hated anxiety. Why did so many people have to make other's lives miserable?

"Maybe she stole them." Eva's red lipstick almost disappeared with the tightening of her lips.

Her tone cast a hint of fear, which only added to Calley's concern. She wasn't about to let on that she'd seen the same person outside her apartment that morning. Eva was already over-protective. This would only make her worse.

"It doesn't matter what she wants," Eva said. "There's no way she's getting in that door." After a kid high on drugs robbed the store several months ago, she bought a state-of-the-art alarm system, complete with a locked door and buzzer to allow entrance.

Most burglars didn't bother with their small shop. The E. Martinez Gallery of Fine Used Art sold paintings on consignment and not from any world-renowned artists. They kept only a small amount of cash in the drawer. The guy who'd robbed the store months before walked away with a whopping sixteen dollars, ten of which came from Calley's purse.

Calley turned back to the window. Nothing about the woman's appearance stuck out except the five-hundred-dollar boots. Similar Brave's caps were owned by thousands in the area, and the jacket was something you could pick up at any local department store.

The stranger looked up, and her eyes met Calley's. She seemed unfazed that anyone was aware of her presence. Her lack of concern unnerved Calley. The microwave dinged, causing Calley to jump.

"She has an evil stare." Eva walked back to the kitchen area. "You know what they say. The eyes are the window to the soul. Her eyes tells me she's an unhappy lady."

Calley's belly fluttered like small wings of an angel. She patted the growing lump at her midsection. "Don't worry. I'll make sure nothing happens to you. Not even five months and already active. Just like your father." She joined Eva in the back.

"Too bad most of his activity involved screwing around." Eva poured liquid creamer into her instant coffee. The aroma of almonds covered the small kitchen space.

The moment Peter Jameson found out about the baby, he announced he was married and wanted nothing more to do with her or their unborn child. Calley lowered herself into a rolling chair behind her desk a few feet from the small refrigerator. Tears formed at the rim of her eyes. She had to stop this. She'd cried way too much for a man who turned out to be a loser.

"I'm sorry. That was cold of me." Eva pushed her wavy brown hair over her shoulder and walked over to Calley. "You'll be fine. And you'll make a great mom." She took a sip of coffee and sat down on the edge of the desk. "I could have finished up on the Nelson sale. You didn't need to come in."

"That's okay. I also wanted to check on the shipment to Monterey before I left." Calley didn't particularly want to go to her cousin's bridal shower. If she hadn't found a couple of shirts to cover her belly, it would have been out of the question.

"I don't know what I'd do without you. You're not only a good worker, but you did the one thing I swore I'd never allow." She paused. "You became more than an employee. You're a friend. And as such, I want you to know that I plan to buy a crib for that baby of yours."

"That is so nice of you." Calley rose and gave Eva a hug. Her closeness to her boss helped Calley's longing for a stronger relationship with her own sister. Eva kept her from feeling alone.

She sat back down while Eva returned to the kitchen for a snack. "We can put it together when it comes in after in a month or two."

"You're so good to me."

"Would you like something?" Eva pulled a paper towel off the roll.

"No, thanks." Nausea from earlier had finally dissipated, by why take chances?

"You've heard absolutely nothing from Peter about getting his medical history?"

"Nothing. I even tried his cell, but it's disconnected." Calley sighed. "I'm not sure it's worth worrying about."

"Probably not."

Calley opened her top drawer and pulled out the picture. She ran her hand over the cold glass of the photograph. A dark-haired man smiled back at her. "Peter, why did you have to be such a jerk? Worse yet, why didn't I figure it out sooner?"

"Now, don't blame yourself." Eva sat down at her own desk on the other wall of the shop. "My husband had an affair, and I never knew it until the woman called me. It took us years of therapy to regain our trust."

"It's just hard to have new dreams when the old ones died out the way they did."

Calley returned a glimpse back out the window. Their watcher looked up and down the road. What could she want? Calley prayed when she headed to Lincolnville in the next hour, the woman wouldn't follow her.

RILEY OWENS SAT IN the sheriff's cruiser parked, along the side of the old highway. Why'd he agree to be best man? He'd have to give the toast, which meant getting up in front of all those people. The blank paper stared up at him. Maybe he should try for something funny. "Like I've got a sense of humor. I'll just make more of a fool out of myself."

He tugged at his collar. June had just arrived, and the air was already stifling. He could only imagine how hot summer would be.

A blue Nissan Versa whizzed by. According to the radar, it was doing sixty-five in the fifty mile per hour zone. Riley, thankful for the distraction, switched on his lights and siren and pulled out behind it. Less than a mile up, the car jerked into the parking lot of Fred's Diner, the local greasy spoon. It pulled into a spot at the front of the building. Riley used his car to block the vehicle from backing up. A dark-haired woman jumped out of the driver's side door.

"Stop right there." Riley placed his hand on his holster, holding the Glock he carried as he emerged from his vehicle. The brunette didn't look dangerous, but you couldn't be sure.

"I need to use the restroom."

"You'll have to hold it until I get finished."

"I can't." Her hands trembled when she wiped her forehead.

"Too bad." He wrote her tag number down and called it in. The name on the registration information read Calley Regan of Atlanta,

Georgia. From the DMV photo, she was the brunette. There were no warrants out for her. Riley figured there was nothing to worry about from the lady, but he'd keep his guard up just in case.

"Good morning, Sheriff. What's new?" Dolly Swenson strolled up behind him. Dolly, a server at Fred's, must have been arriving for the opening shift. The diner was opened for lunch and dinner during the week. It opened for breakfast on the weekend. She lived just a block down and usually walked to work. "Oh, she's a pretty one."

Riley's jaw tightened. "Doesn't matter how pretty they are if they're breaking the law." He pulled his ticket pad from the console in his car.

"You really need to learn how to have fun, Riley. A smart man would find out if she's married, and if not, ask her to lunch." She headed to the woman standing beside the car. "Don't let the old curmudgeon bother you. He sees everything in black or white."

Calley Regan nodded her head and glanced to the road she'd been on. The concern on her face redirected Riley's attention to the street, but no one came or went.

"I need to see your license." He walked up and joined both women. A glance in the driver's side door showed a bottle of water in the console and a pack of opened saltines on the passenger seat.

"Can you write the ticket while I go inside?" Calley handed the license to him. "I promise I won't crawl out the bathroom window."

"This'll take just a minute," he said. Riley wrote up the ticket for speeding. "Sign here." He passed her license back. Dolly continued to watch, obviously disapproving, if her hands on her hips were any indication.

Calley let out a heavy breath and swallowed hard. Her face was pale and sweat covered her forehead. Her hands shook as she signed her name.

"Are you on something?" That would explain her almost paranoid search of Plaskett Drive.

She rolled her eyes. "Prenatal vitamins. And if you don't let me go in, I'm going to throw up all over you."

"I suggest you listen to her, Riley," Dolly said with a laugh. "I know how terrible morning sickness can get, and when you need to hurl, there's no stopping you."

Riley looked into Calley's hazel eyes. "I would think if it were that bad, she'd have stopped sooner. Besides, what kind of mother drives like a maniac and puts her unborn child at risk?"

Calley took a step toward him. "Why you patronizing son of..." She lurched and turned to the side. Not far enough. She threw up on Riley's polished black boots.

"She warned you." Dolly placed an arm around Calley's shoulder. "Come on, dear. Let's get you out of this heat." She paused and turned to Riley. "If you need her, she'll be inside with me. I can't imagine at this point you'd have a problem with that."

Dolly didn't wait for an answer. She led Calley into the diner, out of Riley's view. He shook his left boot. The smell was rancid. He almost thought she'd gotten sick on purpose. That was fine with him. He tore the hefty ticket from the book and slapped it on her windshield.

"I CAN'T BELIEVE I JUST threw up on a cop." Calley shook her head. He wasn't even bad looking. In fact, he was hot. His black cowboy hat sat on top of his forehead. Those dark brown eyes stared down at her, and the day's growth of beard look good on him. His features were strong, from his square jaw to his muscular biceps. She would have enjoyed the view any other time, but the baby had been upsetting her stomach on the hour and a half drive up.

"You really have good timing, don't you?" She talked to the child in her belly.

Country music played from a speaker overhead. Calley sang along. She glanced around the diner while she waited for the woman with the nametag of Dolly to return. Hand-written ads painted on the window announced the special that day. A half pound burger, fries and a coke for three ninety-nine. The thought of that much food made bile rise in Calley's system. She was grateful they hadn't started cooking yet. Greasy food would have only made her feel worse.

She sat off to the right in the first red booth by the door. The vinyl covering was cool to her bare legs. Red stools aligned the counter to her left. Dolly had gone into the back to what Calley assumed was the kitchen area. Voices sounded behind the swinging door. The place reminded her of a small café she'd worked in when she was sixteen. Different color scheme, but same layout.

A black sedan drove past. Calley's hands trembled. She had seen the car in her rearview mirror several times on the interstate. She was sure it had been following her.

"Here you go." Dolly returned from the back room with a cup, drawing Calley's attention from the window. "It's peppermint tea. I drank it when I was pregnant with my second. He gave me a fit during my entire pregnancy." She slid the cup across the table.

"How many kids do you have?" The aroma of mint filled Calley's senses. She drank a sip of the hot liquid.

"Three. All boys." Dolly scooted into the booth across from Calley with a cup of coffee. "This is your first, isn't it?"

"It's obvious I don't know what I'm doing?"

"No, just deductive reasoning. You have no car seat in the back for another kid. What brings you through Lincolnville?"

The tea helped calm Calley's stomach. "My cousin's getting married, and her shower is this weekend."

"My word. You're Lydia's cousin." Dolly patted Calley's hand. "She's just the sweetest thing in the world. No one deserves to be happier than her."

"Yeah." Calley swallowed hard. That's the problem with small towns. Everyone knows everyone else. "Can I ask you a favor?"

"Sure."

"Can you not say anything about the baby? My family doesn't know yet. And seeing as how they're such good Christians, and I'm not married, it's probably not going to go over real big."

"Now don't you worry, I won't tell anyone. And Lydia's a great lady. She isn't the judgmental type."

"It's not Lydia I'm worried about. It's the minister she's marrying."

RILEY FINISHED CLEANING his boots. His mood had gone from bad to worse. He didn't care if Calley Regan was pregnant. He should have locked her up for throwing up on him, if only to confirm his reputation as being cold and heartless. Vomiting on him in front of one of the town gossips didn't help matters. It was probably all over town by now.

"You okay?" BJ stuck her head into his bedroom. "I know you're not thrilled about the people being here for the shower, but it's only the weekend. Then the wedding. After that, you can go back to being the recluse you love to be."

Riley's aunt had a way of being direct with everyone, especially him. She'd raised him after his parents died in a car accident when he was eleven. He brought her up to live after his uncle's death, about six months ago.

"I told you it was fine."

"Your words say fine, but your face has that sourpuss look on it. You need to cheer up, my boy. There should be some nice-looking women at this shower. I understand she's invited her whole sorority from college. If you'd loosen up, you might find one whose company you enjoy."

"I have too much work to worry about chasing after women." Riley didn't want another woman. He hadn't protected the one he'd had before. Why take a chance on losing another?

BJ sat down on the bed. "It's been years since Beth's death. I wish you'd talk to that preacher friend of yours about it so you can move on."

Riley stared at his reflection in the mirror as he adjusted his tie. He had moved on, just not in the way most people thought he should. "I don't need to talk to Matthew about anything. Like you said, it was a long time ago."

"If you say so." A knock on the door interrupted their conversation. "Sounds like our first guests have arrived." She walked from the bedroom and pulled the door partially closed.

BJ's beaming face told of her excitement. She'd probably been bored since she moved from Jacksonville. There certainly were no dinner theatres and the closet large mall was just shy of an hour away. Riley wondered if it was wise uprooting her from her life.

"Well, hello. How are you?" The enthusiasm in BJ's voice carried into the bedroom.

"Hi. You must be BJ. My name's Calley Regan. I think I'm supposed to be here for the weekend."

Riley's stomach bounced. Of all the luck. He glanced through the crack of his opened bedroom door. Her color had returned to her face. He hadn't realized how pretty she was when they'd first met.

"I have two more things in the car," she said.

"You must have planned for every occasion."

"Yeah, I pack a lot. What can I say? I'm a girl." Calley's eyes sparkled.

"A woman can never have too many supplies." BJ gave her a quick hug. "Why don't you bring in the rest? I'll take this one to your room. It's the second on the right."

Riley watched BJ walk into the hallway. He'd found out earlier through the grapevine that he'd given a ticket to Lydia's cousin. That probably wouldn't go over very big since Riley was the best man for her wedding.

Right now, he'd like to find a quick means of escape, but decided Calley should be the one uncomfortable, not him. A fading scent caught his attention when he entered the living room. Calley must have put on perfume before she got to the house. The aroma lingered after she returned outside. At the diner, he hadn't noticed it. He couldn't place the fragrance; he just knew he liked it.

He walked up to the large picture window and watched Calley head to her car. She glanced up and down the road, definitely looking for someone. Her head followed a black car speeding past. It slowed. She continued to watch. Riley came into full view of the window and the vehicle sped off. Maybe she had a fight with her boyfriend.

He returned his attention to Calley, who tugged a guitar case and another suitcase out of the car's trunk. She shouldn't be carrying those heavy items in her condition.

He sucked in a deep breath and headed for the door.

This is the end of Chapter 1 of *Catch Your Breath*. To read more, order on your favorite retailer.

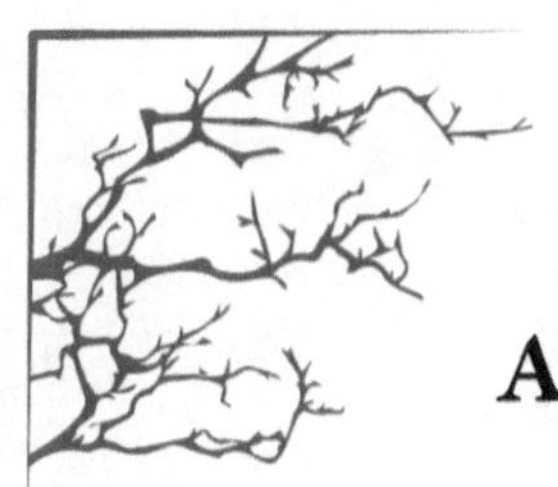

About the Author

Kathryn J. Bain's first release *Breathless* came out January 13, 2012. She has won several awards for her writing including First Place in the International Digital Awards (IDA), First Place in the Royal Palm Literary Awards, Second and Third Place in the Heart of Excellence Readers' Choice Contest, and more.

She became a bestselling author in 2020 when her book *The Chain You Forge* hit number one under Amazon's Holiday Fiction category and stayed there for four days.

She is the former President of Florida Sisters in Crime and Public Relations Director and Membership Director for Ancient City Romance Authors.

She has been a paralegal for over thirty years and works for an attorney who specializes in elder law.

Kathryn grew up in Coeur d'Alene, Idaho. In 1981, she moved to Boise, but it apparently wasn't far enough south, because two years later she headed Jacksonville, Florida and has lived in the sunshine ever since.

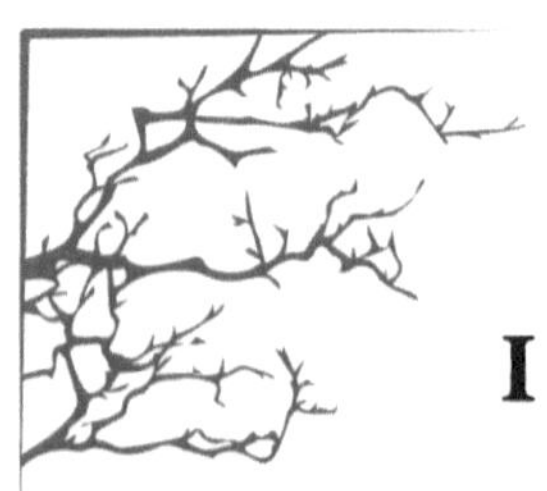

I Need Your Help

1. Write a review. It doesn't have to be elaborate, just something as simple as "I really liked this book."

2. Share my books with your friends and on social media. Word of mouth works better for book sales than any form of advertisement.

3. Post of picture of you reading one of my books and tag me on Facebook or Twitter. (Or your dog, cat, horse, etc.)

Other Available Titles from Kathryn J. Bain

<u>THE KT MORGAN SHORT SUSPENSE SERIES</u>

A Touch of Suspense (Vol. 1-3 of the KT Morgan Short Suspense Series), pub. 2017

The Visitor, pub. 2014

Small Town Terror, pub. 2015

The Reunion, pub. 2016

Run Away, pub. 2019

The Game, pub. 2020

Sucker Punched, pub. 2021

<u>OTHER FICTION BOOKS</u> available

Fade to the Edge, 2019

The Chain You Forge, 2017, #1 Bestseller in Holiday Fiction

Beautiful Imperfection, 2013, Harborlight Books

Game of Hearts, 2012, Astraea Press.

<u>The Lincolnville Mystery Series</u>
Breathless, pub. 2012
Catch Your Breath, pub. 2012
One Last Breath, pub. 2014.
Take Her Breath Away, 2016

<u>MIDDLE-GRADE</u>
Seven Sisters Road, co-written with Jessi Bain, pub. 2020